HARD TICKET TO HAWAII

A NOVELIZATION BY
BRAD CARTER

BASED ON THE SCREENPLAY BY
ANDY SIDARIS

Encyclopocalypse Publications
www.encyclopocalypse.com

Foreword

This is it. This is the one.

The peak of the Sidaris Cinematic Universe.

The *Citizen Kane* of rocket launchers, killer snakes, remote-controlled helicopters, and death by razor Frisbee.

Hard Ticket to Hawaii is that late-night cable movie you stumbled into as a kid, a teen, a barely-sober college student with a pizza on your lap and a questionable beverage in your hand. The one that kept getting better every time you watched it, even if you could never quite explain why.

Was it the rocket launcher in the Jeep?

The snake that burst out of the toilet?

The two agents in bikinis, always outsmarting the bad guys and occasionally out of their own clothes?

Yes. All of that and something extra.

There's a wild sincerity to *Hard Ticket* that no other B-movie ever quite matched. Andy Sidaris didn't make "trash cinema." He made genre films with style, with joy, and with a wink that said he knew exactly what he was doing. This wasn't accidental. It was a cocktail of nunchucks, machine guns, rocket launchers, and beautiful women who actually get the job done.

As I've aged along with the film, and especially after a long afternoon conversation with the lovely Arlene Sidaris about these films, I'm confident this was the secret: Sidaris's films give the women the power.

Donna and Taryn aren't sidekicks. They're not damsels. They fly the plane. They make the plans. They take the shots. They're smart, gorgeous, fully capable and often the only adults in the room, surrounded by men who are mostly shirtless, clueless, or both.

So when we asked Brad Carter to take on this novelization, we knew it had to walk the same tightrope: absurd but never mocking. Sleazy, but never hollow. Carter absolutely delivered. He pulls the pin on the grenade, rides the Malibu Express to Molokai, and cranks out a story just as blood-soaked, bonkers, and sneakily self-aware as the original film.

He even made the snake scarier. I didn't think that was possible.

So buckle up. The blow-up doll is loaded. The secret message is hidden in a sandwich. The Abilene family legacy rolls on. And the 1980s are back—louder, weirder, and more fun than ever.

Just how we like it.

Sean Duregger
Managing Editor
Encyclopocalypse Publications

HARD TICKET TO HAWAII

Chapter One

Dr. Theodore Huang and his team spent three days traipsing through the Amazon rainforest before they finally caught up to the snake. They found it just after it had consumed an entire feral pig. Its massive appetite sated, the snake was sluggish, its natural aggression temporarily tamed as its digestive processes began the slow task of digesting three hundred pounds of pork.

They spotted the snake in the underbrush approximately two miles inland from the river. It was stretched out to its full length, which Dr. Huang estimated to be near twenty feet. It appeared pregnant, its belly distended as the recently devoured pig made its journey through the snake's digestive system. Truly a wonder of nature, this a majestic beast, and one that would fetch top dollar from Dr. Huang's carefully vetted buyers. The bidding would open at a million dollars, the doctor decided. This was no house pet, after all.

"That's it," the doctor said, calling the group to a halt. "Over there, in that shallow depression."

A low murmur from the trio of hired men answered him. The tenor of their mutterings was closer to awe than fear. After all, these men were seasoned jungle guides. They encountered deadly wildlife on a near daily basis. But they still had a healthy respect for these dangerous animals. And this snake was as dangerous as they came. Since escaping from an underground biotech facility in Sao Paolo, the snake had cut a deadly swath through the rainforest. At least two indigenous tribes had been decimated by the unusually cunning and intelligent predator.

"Don't worry," one of the men said. "We get him, no problem."

"Are you sure?" Dr. Huang asked. "Because you nearly walked right past it. You three are supposed to be good at this sort of thing, yet it was the Harvard-educated tenderfoot that actually spotted the animal."

"I said we get him," the man answered. "We get him."

He was a tough, leathery looking man named Igor who had a reputation for fearlessness. At his signal, the two other men placed the crate they'd been carrying on the ground. It was made of thick wooden slats and had holes drilled into it at regularly spaced intervals. If all went according to plan, the snake would remain in a similar crate for the entirety of its voyage from the rainforest to whoever was lucky enough to win the auction.

The two men looked to Igor, who nodded his approval. They regarded him with some amount of reverence as they fell in behind him as he crept toward the snake's hiding place.

"Remember," Dr. Huang said, "the specimen must not be damaged."

"*Si, si,*" Igor said, glancing back over his shoulder. He turned to the other two men and whispered something in their native tongue.

Dr. Huang stepped back and let his assistants do the dirty work. They were paid to take risks. And it wasn't as if their deaths would be any great lost in the grand scheme of things. They were simple men who made their living as fishing guides on the Amazon River. They could be snuffed out of existence with little consequence to the world at large. Dr. Huang, on the other hand, was one of the preeminent minds in the field of bioweapons technology. It was his considered opinion that his premature death would have a lasting impact on the future of any number of sovereign nations. So he stayed well away from the massive reptile and let his hired simpletons capture the snake.

They used standard animal wrangling equipment: a pair of catch poles similar to those used by dog catchers and a large black burlap sack. At Igor's signal, both men dropped the plastic nooses at the end of the catch poles around the snake's blunt oblong head. For a moment, it appeared that the arduous trek through the jungle would culminate in an anticlimax. The snake didn't even twitch as the two men carefully tightened the nooses. It regarded them with glassy black eyes, its forked tongue flicking in and out of its mouth.

Igor circled in front of the snake. He spoke to his two assistants in hushed tones as he held the burlap bag before him. So far, everything was proceeding according to plan. Once the snake was hooded, it would become disoriented and even easier to handle. They'd load the snake into the crate and carry it back to their campsite. By tomorrow, it would be safely packed into the cargo hold of Dr. Huang's plane and bound for his lab in Guam.

Yes, things were going smoothly. And that's why Dr. Huang's belly seemed to be full of butterflies. In his experience, things often went quite smoothly right before they erupted into chaos. He swept back the hem of his vest and pulled his gun from its holster. The gun was loaded with tranquilizer darts carrying a narcotic load potent enough to send the snake to dreamland. The gun was a last resort. Had the snake been a normal animal, sure, the tranquilizer darts would be safe and effective. But this was no normal snake, and there was no way of predicting how it would react in any situation.

"Carefully," he reminded the men. "Carefully, please."

"*Si, si,*" Igor replied.

The snake was a mutant mongrel. Its genetic makeup was a

melting pot of deadly reptile DNA, a mingling of a dozen different constrictors and vipers. As if its ancestry hadn't made it dangerous enough, the snake carried a contagious strain of cancer born in the bowels of a clandestine lab owned by a top-secret military contractor. Now, it wasn't as much a reptile as a slithering, semi-sentient killing machine, full of venom and disease.

And that killing machine bided its time, waiting until Igor had begun to lower the black bag over its head. Then, with a movement so violent and abrupt that it tore the catch poles from the hands of the two men, the snake struck. It buried its fangs in Igor's forearm. The other two men scrambled to get ahold of the catch poles, but that task was made impossible by the furious combat between Igor and the snake.

Howling with pain and outrage as he struggled to free his arm, Igor collapsed to the ground. He battered the snake's head with his fist to no avail. With a swiftness that belied its distended belly, the snake coiled itself around Igor, wrapping him from chest to ankles in its sleek, brightly patterned length. Muscles rippled beneath the snake's shiny hide.

"Good Lord!" Dr. Huang was too impressed to be afraid.

The other two men, however, were terrified. They'd finally managed to grab the catch poles and were pulling them in opposite directions. Although the snake gave no indication that it was in distress, Dr. Huang worried that the two idiots might strangle their quarry.

"Step aside," he commanded, raising his tranquilizer pistol and taking aim.

The men were all too eager to obey. They dropped the poles and danced back, putting distance between themselves and the bloody spectacle unfolding before them. And it had indeed become bloody. Igor's screams died abruptly as the snake coiled and tightened around him. There was a sound like dry tree limbs snapping, and Dr. Huang knew that the man's ribs, and possibly his spine, had been broken. Igor's eyes rolled back in their sockets. His neck bulged as he convulsed. Thick white foam and blood ran from his mouth. The snake's venom had begun its work in earnest, attacking Igor's central nervous system. Dr. Huang supposed this was merciful.

At least Igor would be quite beyond pain by now.

He fired two darts into the snake's bulging midsection, then stepped back and waited for the sedatives to take effect. After two uncomfortable minutes, the beast finally slipped into unconsciousness. Its hold on Igor gradually loosened until its coiled body went slack. When Igor's corpse rolled onto the muddy ground, it looked like a flattened tube of toothpaste. The jagged tips of his broken ribs protruded at odd angles from his torso. A length of intestine dangled from one of the wounds. In a matter of seconds, the first scavenging insects emerged from their hiding places. They swarmed over the corpse, eager to get their fill before the larger scavengers arrived on the scene. Igor's partners, these supposedly hardened jungle explorers, gagged and puked into the bushes.

Dr. Huang shrugged. Very few expeditions went off without a hitch. Sometimes the hiccups were relatively minor. Other times, it went this way. There was no limit to the cruelty of the natural world. Dr. Huang realized this dictum sounded philosophical, but he knew that it was really just a simple statement of fact.

He waited for the men to get themselves under control, then gave the order to load the sleeping snake into the crate and begin the long march back to civilization.

Chapter Two

Donna Hamilton stayed in the water until the sun disappeared below the horizon. Once it was too dark to watch the fish moving through the water like multihued jewels, she popped the snorkel out of her mouth and climbed up the ladder to the aft deck of the *Malibu Express*. It was a 35-foot yacht currently occupying a slip at the Blue Sky Yacht Club, and for the last two weeks, it had been Donna's home.

As soon as she set foot on deck, she found herself encircled by the arms of her sometime boyfriend, Rowdy Abilene.

"You know, we could get back in the water," she suggested. "Do a little night swimming..."

Rowdy pulled her closer. "Are you kidding? I've got better things to do with my body temperature."

And Donna knew exactly what those things were. For the past two weeks, she and Rowdy had engaged in those body temperature-intensive activities with a wild abandon that rivaled the jackrabbits of Rowdy's native West Texas. Thirteen glorious days of sunshine and cruising along the coast. Thirteen nights of lovemaking so intense and passionate that it fogged up the windows of the yacht's single bedroom. And in the morning, it would all come to an end. Donna could hardly believe it had gone by so fast. It seemed like it was only yesterday that Rowdy had met her at the LAX gate. Vacations always seemed to be over too quickly.

They stood on deck, kissing and caressing, until the evening breezed turned cool, then they went inside.

In the morning, she'd board a plane bound for Honolulu. From there, she'd catch a commuter flight to Molokai. And then, it was back to the steady grind of her Agency caseload. The realization that their amorous fortnight was coming to an end had settled between them like a weight, and their conversation hit a lull while Rowdy stepped into the galley to prepare two cups of Earl Grey.

When he emerged with the steaming mugs, Donna told him that she'd had a wonderful time with him and would miss him terribly. The statement came out sounding flippant, but she actually meant it. She loved spending her downtime on Rowdy's yacht. It was pleasant falling asleep and waking up to the sound of gentle waves lapping at the side of the boat. There was nothing more relaxing than sipping a rum drink and watching the sunset from one of the chaise lounges on the aft deck. It was never easy to tear herself away and go back to work. But she knew that the sporadic nature of their relationship was what made it work. What she and Rowdy had was simple and uncluttered. Constant close contact would undoubtedly spoil it sooner or later.

Rowdy passed her a cup of tea and said, "You know, you don't have to go back to Molokai. I could have you detailed to the Los Angeles office."

"Look, we both know the Agency needs me on Molokai. There's been too much time and energy spent on investigating the drug pipeline running through there. The agency has spent years building a case, and we're just now seeing the tip of the iceberg."

Rowdy shook his head. "I just think drug enforcement is no place for a girl as pretty as you."

Donna liked Rowdy—*really* liked him, in fact—but his views on women in law enforcement weren't exactly progressive. She hated having to remind him that her record with the Agency was nearly as distinguished as his. And if she really wanted to touch a nerve, she could always remind him of his poor marksmanship scores. Rowdy's terrible aim was the stuff of Agency legend.

"Let me guess, the next thing out of your mouth will be 'Me Tarzan, you Jane,' right?" She blew the steam off the top of her tea and took a cautious sip. "We've been through this before. I can't just run away from my responsibilities and into your arms, no matter how mind-blowing the sex is."

"Well, I guess you can't blame a guy for trying."

"Yeah? How about you try this?" Donna put her cup of tea on the counter, then reached behind her back to untie her bikini top.

Rowdy took the hint, and they got down to doing what they did best together.

Meanwhile, back on Molokai, Henry Kalani throttled the boat's engine down until it was barely idling. He let the waves push it as close to the beach as possible, then he killed the engine altogether and hopped over the side. Deputy Bobby Hale did likewise, swinging his legs over the side of the boat and splashing into the shallows. The two men dragged the boat—not much more than an inflatable life raft with a small outboard engine—onto the sand. Once Henry was sure they'd gotten the far enough onto the beach to keep it from being dragged out by the tide, he let go and motioned to his deputy.

"Far enough, kid," he said. "We won't be here long enough for the tide to come in."

Yes sir," Bobby answered. "Let me get the shotgun."

"Don't bother. We don't need to lug that thing around. Besides, this is Molokai, not Beirut."

Bobby seemed confused. "But regulations state that when we're doing an inspection…"

"Give it a rest." Henry waved off the deputy's concerns. "You can save that by-the-book stuff for when the boss is around. But right now, he's at his office in Honolulu and we're out here in the boonies. Now come on. We have to hike a bit."

Bobby glanced at the shotgun stowed behind the back seat, then shrugged and followed Henry up the beach and into the woods.

Henry usually made his trips to this part of Molokai alone, but since he was closing in on retirement age, he figured it was time to start giving his deputy more responsibilities. Not that working for the Molokai County Marshall Service carried much responsibility. The US Marshalls' office in Honolulu and the state cops did most of the heavy lifting these days and even that didn't amount to much. Molokai wasn't exactly a hub of criminal activity. There were rumors of a federal undercover investigation being run on the Island, but Henry had never seen any evidence of it. As far as he knew, it was the South Pacific version of Mayberry USA on Molokai. The heaviest action they saw out here was breaking up fights between drunk tourists. Not exactly Dirty Harry shit.

"This part of the island is owned by the Daioo family," Henry explained as they picked their way through the stand of Koa trees. "They been growing weed out here for three generations."

"So we're here to bust them?" Bobby asked. "Then why didn't we bring the shotguns?"

"We're not busting anyone." Henry laughed. "Once or twice a year, I come out here and say, 'Hey, brah, take it easy with the Mary Jane!' Then I hit them with a little fine, plus a little extra for my trouble."

"But you still let them grow it?" Bobby almost sounded indignant.

"Sure, why not? It don't hurt nobody." Henry shrugged. "It means there's jobs for the locals, then the locals spend their money in town. Everybody makes out. I get a little package for myself. You know, just to pass around and make friends. Remember, I'm retiring in a month. You're going to be number one around here real soon, so you better start learning this routine."

"Yeah, okay," Bobby said. "But what about that undercover operation the feds are running on the island?"

Henry laughed. "Come on, kid. If there was a federal investigation, they would have taken down the Daioo family on day one. Don't believe every rumor you hear."

They emerged from the forest into a small clearing where two large greenhouses stood. The place was a hive of activity. At least a dozen people were hard at work, loading boxes into onto a truck, carrying supplies, and doing assorted tasks that Henry couldn't begin to guess at.

"Damn..." Bobby whistled softly. "I thought you said this was just a small family operation."

Henry grabbed his deputy and tugged him behind a nearby tree. "Shut up, kid. Something doesn't seem right."

It was more than just a feeling he had. There were guys he didn't recognize circulating among the workers. Although these strangers wore floral print shirts and cut-off trousers, they sure as hell weren't local. Their complexions were too pasty for them to have spent much time on the beach. These dudes were from the mainland. And they were packing heat. Like serious heat too. Military hardware, automatic weapons. Henry didn't care for this one bit.

"Look at all that work," Bobby whispered. "And you see those white guys carrying machine guns? What the hell is going on here?"

Henry didn't know the answer to that question, and he had

no intention of poking his nose into things. Whatever the Daioo family was up to, whoever they'd gotten into bed with, those were matters best left to the boys in Honolulu.

"Come on, kid." Henry grabbed Bobby's arm. "Let's get back to the boat."

The deputy looked like he was gearing up for an argument.

"I said let's get our asses back to the boat," Henry insisted.

Bobby must have heard the urgency in his voice, because he followed Henry back into the small patch of forest. They'd made it most of the way through—the boat was in sight—when they stumbled over a tripwire. Snares of rough rope cinched tight around their ankles. A hidden system of pulleys and counterweights squeaked as the ropes went taut. In a matter of seconds, the two Marshals were jerked from the ground and hoisted upside down. They dangled in the air like a pair of piñatas at a child's birthday party.

"What the hell, man?" Bobby yelped.

Three men stepped from behind the trees and stood there, laughing at the Marshals' predicament.

"Come on, this ain't funny," Henry said, trying to summon every ounce of authority he possessed as he demanded to be let down. "Go ask Herman Daioo who I am. He'll tell you."

The three men laughed. They were a motley crew that were clearly up to no good. One was a white dude with soap opera-styled blonde hair. He wore a pair of mirrored sunglasses carried a double-barreled shotgun, holding it against his chest like it was some fragile heirloom. He was flanked on one side by another blonde-haired white guy, this one with a horseshoe mustache on his face and an Uzi in his hand. On the other side of the guy with shades was the trio's token islander. He was a big boy with an earring dangling from his left earlobe.

Henry cleared his throat and tried again. "I said you better let us down. I'm a friend of the Daioo family. Go ask them."

"I'd love to ask them," the guy with the shades said. "But I can't communicate with the dead. Maybe you can ask them when you see them in hell."

He brought the shotgun to his shoulder and fired twice. The first shot hit Henry square in the gut and spun him around. The second took poor Bobby's head right off his shoulders.

Shit, that ain't cool, Henry thought as his mouth flooded with hot blood. *I was just about to retire, brah.*

As his vision began to dim, he heard the three men laugh.

"You got both of 'em, Shades. Good shooting!" one of them said.

The man with the sunglasses broke open his shotgun and plucked the spent shells. "Cut these two assholes down. Run them and their boat through the shredder, then feed them to the fish."

Henry didn't like the sound of that at all. What the hell kind of shredder did they have out here? Thankfully, he didn't think he'd be around long enough to find out.

Chapter Three

Glen Dickson watched as three men worked at breakneck speed to unload the contents of their plane into the warehouse. They had the look of a crew that had been working together for a while. Not only was their system smooth as silk, but they did it without speaking a single word. Each guy had a job, and he did it. Glen signed off on the bill of lading and watched the three men pile back into the plane and fly off to the next job. All told, they were in and out of the warehouse in under ten minutes.

"Wonder if those boys would be interested in working here?" he wondered aloud.

His workforce—foremen included—were just coming back from their third coffee break of the morning. Glen heard them before he saw them. That's how loud they were grumbling about having to actually do something productive.

"Man, you think those guys could have dropped any more boxes on us?" Luke whined.

"Yeah, must be a hundred of them," Jimbo agreed.

Glen sighed. These were his two foremen, for crying out loud. If he couldn't count on them to be anything other than lazy and unmotivated, what hope was there for the rest of the crew?

My own fault, Glen reminded himself. That's what I get for hiring family.

His life would improve immediately if he could just fire his idiot nephews. He believed this to his core. Luke and Jimbo were as incompetent as they were shiftless, and that meant they couldn't be trusted to do anything without constant supervision. And that in turn meant there was a serious lack of efficiency at the warehouse of the Molokai Cargo Company. All because Glen couldn't tell his baby sister Tammy no. Easier to deal with the constant headaches and heartburn than have to deal with her bitching.

While he waited for his nephews and the other workers to return from their break, Glen flipped through the bill of lading. As usual, there was a hodgepodge of stuff in the delivery. Some was ultimately bound for the mainland, while some of it went to the other islands. Nearly all of it occupied some sort of legal grey area. After all, there had to be some reason people used Molokai Cargo instead of the boys in brown or the good old postal service. Something did jump out at him, however: this shipment contained not one but two exotic animals, specifically snakes. One was bound for the wildlife institute on Molokai; the other was headed for the big island and ultimately to Guam. The former was an endangered species, while the latter was only described as "Dangerous/Use Caution While Handling."

Glen checked these two crates, just to make sure they had adequate ventilation. He didn't peek through the air holes. For one thing, he'd long ago given up being curious about what passed through his warehouse. In fact, the less he knew, the better. For another, he hated snakes. Goddamn things gave him the heebie-jeebies.

"Okay, geniuses!" he called. "This load ain't gonna sort itself! Get to work!"

There was more of the usual grumbling, but the men fanned out in search of their hard hats, gloves, and all the other OSHA-mandated bullshit.

Glen grabbed Luke and Jimbo before they could get lost in the shuffle. "Listen, we got a couple live animals in this shipment. I want you jackasses to make sure they pass through here unharmed, okay? We got a reputation to uphold."

"Yeah, what reputation is that?" Jimbo asked.

Glen slapped him on the back of the head. "Don't crack wise with me, kid. I'd hate to be forced to drag you out behind the warehouse and kick your ass in front of your crew. Now, can you handle this one simple task or do I need to give you step-by-step instructions?"

They mumbled something that sounded like an affirmative. Glen knew from experience that was the best answer he was going to get out of these two numbskulls.

Later, when he had a chance to think it over, he'd understand that this was where he went wrong. Trusting these two honor roll students to handle the snakes without getting them mixed up was, without a doubt, a world class blunder on his part. Despite this acknowledgement, he wouldn't fire them. It just wasn't worth facing Tammy's wrath, Glen decided. Thanksgiving dinner was tense enough as it was.

Donna arrived at her bungalow on Molokai just in time to catch her roommate, Taryn Foster, returning from her morning swim. Donna parked her Jeep on the gravel driveway, climbed out, and watched Taryn, clad in a white bikini and dripping seawater, trot across the patchy grass. Taryn was, like Donna, a blonde with the sort of body that a cultured man might call "luscious" or "nubile," and those less poetically inclined would refer to as "so fucking hot" or "smoking" or something similar. One could be forgiven for thinking the two women were sisters, and in fact, Donna did think of Taryn as a younger, somewhat naïve sibling.

"These early morning hours are killing me," Taryn gasped as

she jogged by Donna and headed for the outdoor shower attached to a tree in the front yard. It wasn't much more than a shower head hooked up to a garden hose, but Donna thought it wasn't bad for a weekend DIY project.

"Drug enforcement agents can't afford to be soft," Donna laughed.

"I'm supposed to be soft," Taryn replied. "I'm a woman."

"Yeah, and if it wasn't for this arrangement, you'd be a dead woman," Donna reminded her.

Taryn squealed as the first spray of cold water hit her. When she recovered, she said, "At least when I testified against the mob in Vegas, they threatened to kill me quickly. You're taking your sweet time."

Whenever Taryn started to complain about her living situation, Donna reminded herself that Taryn was actually an incredibly brave woman. She'd taken the stand as a witness in two separate federal trials. One of those trials sent Vito DiPrince away for life and the other sent Jimmy "The Nose" Giardino to lockdown for a twenty-five year stretch. Her testimony had been the nail in the coffin for both gangsters, and the fallout for Taryn's personal life had been immense. During the trial, there had been no fewer than five attempts on her life. After the convictions came down, the Agency thought it was best to stash her in the WitSec program, somewhere off the beaten path but with a constant agency presence. So Vivian Simoneaux-DiPrince, one-time mob mistress, became Taryn Foster, resident of the island of Molokai, roommate of Agent Donna Spears, and, most recently, an agent in training.

"Look, Taryn, you didn't make such a bad deal with our witness protection program."

"Well..." Taryn wriggled out of her bikini top. She did a slow spin under the spray of water. "At least I'm in the islands, right?"

"That's the spirit," Donna said.

Taryn shut off the water and headed for the house. Donna followed.

They were officially on duty in an hour, which was more than enough time for them to freshen up and get into their work clothes. In their case, work clothes were khaki shorts and matching sleeveless shirts, accompanied by boots that looked like they belonged in the Australian outback. Ridiculous, of course, but it was the feminine riff on the Molokai Cargo Company's pilot uniform. Glen Dickson, the boss man at MCC wasn't a proponent of women's lib, apparently.

After she was dressed and ready for work, Donna grabbed a cup of coffee to help stave off the jetlag, then headed outside to wait for Taryn. The latter always needed an extra few minutes to make sure her hair and makeup were just right. She may have been an agent in training, but she still possessed the vanity of a Vegas showgirl. Donna cut her some slack in that department. After all, WitSec wasn't just a relocation program. It was a complete identity overhaul. New name, new address, new job, new person. It was like doing an undercover job that lasted forever. With all that taken into account, Taryn's adjustment had been nothing short of miraculous. A few extra minutes spent applying makeup and hairspray were a small concession to make.

Donna leaned against the front of the Jeep and tried not to let her thoughts drift to Rowdy Abilene as she looked at the sparkling blue expanse of the Pacific Ocean. She'd always known that he wasn't the settling down type, and that suited her just fine. After all, she wasn't exactly the domestic type either. Still, it would be nice to see him more than a couple times a year. The sound of the front door banging shut snapped her out of her reverie.

"Hey, Donna, when the Agency offered me this gig living in Hawaii and helping you keep your cover, it sounded like paradise." Taryn said as she emerged from the house. "But you never let up. All these workouts are killing me. I'm sore all over."

"The Agency expects us to be fit at all times," Donna replied, climbing into the Jeep.

"But I'm still technically a civilian." Taryn hopped into the passenger seat. For someone who claimed to be sore all over, she was moving just fine.

"Hey, that doesn't mean you can't be buff."

Donna twisted the key in the ignition. She put the car in gear, paused just long enough to slap her roommate a high-five, then headed for the Molokai Cargo HQ. From there, they'd take the Cessna to haul deliveries to whatever locations were on their itinerary. All in all, it wasn't a bad gig. Donna had done worse. And from what Taryn had told her, so had she. Sure, Glen Dickson had a sideline in small time smuggling, but it was nothing too heavy and they Agency was willing to turn a blind eye. It would be a shame if it turned out that he was somehow mixed up in the drug trade and Molokai Cargo got shut down. Finding new cover IDs would be a drag.

Taryn pushed some buttons on the radio until she landed on a station playing a Pat Benatar tune. She twisted the volume knob until the music could be heard over the wind.

Luke and Jimbo were, like many young men, easily distracted. When the distraction in question involved a pair of beautiful women, that maxim was doubly true. The full consequences of this quality of being easily distracted weren't always immediately apparent.

For instance, when the two hot babe pilots rolled up in their Jeep, there was a single, immediate consequence to the brothers' inattention. As they both craned their necks to get a better view of the two babes walking across the parking lot, they lost control of the handcart full of boxes that they'd been guiding across the loading dock. Several of the wooden crates toppled from the top of the stack and hit the floor. However, their inattention would have further-reaching consequences that weren't readily apparent. The would, as always, reveal themselves in time.

"Holy shit!" Luke yelped. "Would you watch where you're going?"

"Fuck you, man. This one was your fault," Jimbo snapped, jabbing his finger into his brother's chest. "Now help me get this shit loaded back up before Uncle Glen sees."

They got to work, heaving the heavy crates back onto the handcart.

"Shit, some of the labels came off," Luke said, stooping to grab two labels that had pulled loose from their staples when the boxes tumbled. "And look, it's the labels for the snakes. How do we know which label goes on which box?"

Jimbo snatched the labels from his brother's hand and examined them closely, his brow knitting in deep thought. Finally, he shrugged and said, "Who cares? It's snakes, right? One snake is pretty much the same as another."

"I don't know, man. Maybe we should tell Uncle Glen."

Jimbo scoffed at the suggestion. "Fuck that. Last thing I need is him on our backs for the rest of the day. You know Mom keeps saying that he's just looking for an excuse to fire us."

"Yeah," Luke said. "I guess you're right."

Jimbo snatched a stapler off his tool belt and affixed one label to a crate containing a snake. Then he turned to the next crate and repeated the process. The two brothers hefted the crates back to their spot atop the stacked handcart.

"Hey, bro," Luke said as they resumed the process of inching the cart across the loading dock. "You ever wonder if those two blonde broads are lesbos? Uncle Glen said they were roommates. Like maybe they're more than just roommates, huh?"

"I don't need to know what you think about when you jerk

off," Jimbo laughed. Then after a moment's consideration, he added, "That would be hot if they were lesbos, though."

Donna and Taryn punched the clock in the office, then headed out to the tarmac to meet Glen Dickson and get their work orders for the day. Their plane was a single-prop four-seater Cessna. It was perfect to the short hops she and Taryn worked. The cargo hold was small, but that suited their purposes. Small deliveries with a sideline in scenic air tours, those were the bread and butter of the Molokai Cargo Company.

"Hey, ladies," Glen called as he emerged from the warehouse, clipboard in hand. "Ready for today's run?"

"Hey, Mr. Dickson," Donna said. "Yeah, I think we're ready."

"What do you have for us?" Taryn asked.

Their boss slowed his approach as he neared them. He didn't make much of an effort to hide his slow head-to-toe appraisal of his favorite flight team.

"You got one set of honeymooners booked for the Halawa Valley," Glen said, gesturing over his shoulder to a pair of young newlyweds crossing the tarmac with backpacks in hand. "They're camping overnight just east of Kapukahehu."

"Sounds romantic," Donna said.

Taryn disagreed. "Sounds terrible. First week as husband and wife, you gotta do it on the hard ground? Ugh, no thanks."

Glen flipped to the next sheet on his clipboard. "And hey, just one more for today. Looks like you get to transport a snake to Molokai Ranch Wildlife Park. My idiot nephews will come load that sucker up for you."

Right on cue, Luke and Jimbo arrived, bearing a wooden crate. They loaded it into the cargo hold. They newlyweds also strolled up and passed their backpacks to Glen, who situated them atop the snake's crate. They introduced themselves as

Jamie and Joey Gilbert of Shelbyville, Indiana. Donna figured them for a pair of high school sweethearts who'd gone steady through college and then got hitched as soon as graduation was over. They certainly looked like a pair of All-American lovebirds.

"You girls be safe out there," Glen said. He turned to his nephews and gave them a withering look. "Don't think I didn't notice that you dinged that crate. You know, 'Fragile, Handle With Care' isn't just a suggestion. I swear, sometimes I wonder what kind of drugs your mother did while she was pregnant with you."

The uncle and his nephews headed back for the warehouse, grumbling as they went.

"You're going to love this, guys," Donna told the young couple. "The valley is so romantic. Isn't that right, Taryn?"

"It sure is." Taryn nodded, shooting a quick elbow into Donna's ribs. "You guys climb aboard and make yourselves comfortable. There's some sodas and pretzels in the backseat in case you feel like a snack."

The young lovers climbed into the backseat as Donna and Taryn made their final pre-flight inspection of the plane's exterior.

"You know," Taryn said as she checked the wing flaps. "I've figured out a cure for my boredom. I'm just going to pretend I'm in a James Bond movie."

"You've got a great imagination," Donna agreed.

"I guess I still have a whole new identity to develop. And plenty to forget."

Donna leaned against the fuselage. "Okay, out of all the Bond actors, who's your favorite?"

"I'd give them all equal time," Taryn giggled.

Donna shook her head. She favored Roger Moore, herself. But she'd be damned if she let that slip to Taryn. Once she got ahold of information like that, Taryn's teasing could be relentless. One time, after a few drinks, Donna had let it slip that she'd lost her virginity during a Van Halen concert. For the following two weeks, Taryn had blasted "Ain't Talkin' Bout Love" every time they took the Jeep for a drive.

"Come on, secret agent girl," Donna said. "Let's get to work."

They climbed aboard, Donna in the pilot's seat and Taryn beside her as co-pilot. They put on their headsets and waited for the all-clear from the tower.

"This is Cessna Molokai Cargo, November niner-niner-seven-eight-six requesting clearance on runway five left," Donna said into her headset mic.

"Roger, Molokai Cargo." The voice from the tower was clear in her headphones. "You're clear for takeoff."

Donna glanced at Taryn, who smiled and flashed her a thumbs-up.

It didn't take Glen long to figure out how badly his nephews had bungled what should have been the simplest task of the day. He was walking the loading dock, checking the outgoing cargo for broken customs seals, missing labels, or bad routing information when he discovered that the pair of idiots had loaded the wrong snake onto the Cessna. There was no warning label on the remaining Live Snake crate. Although the shipping label indicated that this was the snake bound for the Guam office of the United States Department of Health, it wasn't affixed to the correct crate. Further investigation revealed that the label had in fact been removed and then reaffixed with staples. You didn't have to be Sherlock Holmes to connect the dots on this one.

"Luke and Jimbo!" Glen shouted. "Get your asses front and center on the double!"

They slouched out of the rows of shelves, cups of coffee in hand.

"Well?" Glen demanded. "Care to explain how you guys managed to load the wrong goddamn snake on the Cessna?"

"What do you mean?" Jimbo scratched his head. "We put the snake on there."

"Yes, but it was the *wrong* snake." Glen clenched his teeth and forced himself to rein in the urge to strangle the kid. "That crate was stamped with a bright orange 'Biohazard' warning, which I'm assuming you covered when you were putting the label back on it."

Luke shrugged. "Okay, so what? A snake's a snake, right?"

"No, my dear nephew, that's not true at all." Glen's brain conjured up the image of him smashing to the two idiots' skulls together like a pair of coconuts. It was awful tempting to make that brief fantasy a reality as he watched his nephews look at him like he was the one in the wrong. He took a deep breath and continued in the calmest tones he could manage, "The snake you put on that plane was contaminated. It was on its way to Guam."

He left out the part about how the snake was one of Dr. Huang's freakshow oddities that had to make a detour through Molokai Cargo to avoid customs entanglements. Glen didn't make a habit of doing business with smugglers of exotic animals, but Dr. Huang paid handsomely enough that Glen could override his ethical misgivings. After all, the doc was careful, and Glen figured none of this would ever blow back in his face. Until now, that is. At that very moment, the mutant snake was bound for the Molokai Ranch Wildlife Park. Despite the fanciful name, the place housed a wildlife research center. It wouldn't take those egghead scientists long to figure out the snake they'd been sent was no ordinary reptile. The connection between Glen and Dr. Huang—a Department of Health employee with a sideline in exotic animals—wasn't exactly a tangled web, even if Glen had only spoken to the man once.

"Now, I gotta get on the radio and see if I can undo your

mistake," he growled. "I gotta make sure that snake doesn't make it to the wildlife park."

"I still don't get it." Luke looked at his brother, who answered with a shrug.

In the rear cargo hold of the Cessna, the snake slumbered. Nestled into the warm bed of straw at the bottom of the crate, the snake slept so peacefully that a casual observer might have mistaken it for dead. Its brain might have been roughly the size of a walnut, but it nevertheless pulsed with activity, its synapses firing off vividly violent dreams that tickled the snake's pleasure centers.

The dreams were promises the snake made itself, dreams of bloodshed, death, and destruction. And even though the snake's digestive system was still processing the wild boar it consumed in the jungle, its hunger grew with each dreaming moment. And then, roused by the bouncing and jostling of the plane landing on the packed dirt runway, the snake awoke. Its tongue flicked in and out, tasting the chemical trails left behind by the disembarking humans. It listened to the squeaking, creaking, clattering sounds of their departure. And when their strange voices faded to silence, the snake uncoiled and began to probe the crate for weak spots.

The radio emitted a burst of static that startled the snake, but only for a moment. It paused to listen to the tinny voice coming from the crackling speaker.

"This Honolulu calling November niner-niner-seven-eight-six. Come in please."

Chapter Four

The boat's captain—a perpetually nervous and sweaty scoundrel named Frazer Schmidt—cut the engine and made his way aft, where Mr. Chang and his security detail were waiting. Mr. Chang, dressed in a navy blazer and white slacks was watching as his assistant readied the remote control helicopter. The head of his security team, a gargoyle-faced giant covered in slabs of muscle, stood directly behind Mr. Chang. Frazer didn't know the giant's real name. Mr. Chang only referred to him as Destroyer. That should have been a red flag. Frazer should have gotten the hell away from this organization the moment he learned that it employed people who went by those sort of nicknames. What was this, an international drug cartel or some tough guy biker gang? Frazer should have known better. But then again, that was the story of his life. He was smart enough to recognize the error of his ways, but he was seemingly helpless to act any other way. It was a paradox that he'd never managed to unravel.

"Cargo is secure," the assistant said, passing the remote to his boss. "You're clear for takeoff, Mr. Chang."

Frazer fidgeted as he stood nearby. If there had been room to pace on the thirty-foot boat, he'd have done so. But since the aft deck was crowded with Mr. Chang and his coterie of thugs, he settled for shifting his weight from one foot to the other and scratching at the nape of his neck.

"This whole thing still makes me nervous," he said. "I'd almost rather try running it through customs. I got connections there, you know."

"Oh, I should trust these connections of yours and take a gamble on Customs?" Mr. Chang scoffed. "The way they watch us? No, I think not. This has always worked. We don't have to worry about customs or the Coast Guard, and the boys get paid. It's nice and clean. And besides, I do so enjoy piloting this whirlybird."

Frazer knew better than to argue. Mr. Chang wasn't the sort of man who welcomed debate. He was, for lack of a better term, one scary motherfucker. In the three years Frazer had been in Mr. Chang's employ, he'd seen the man order executions without a second thought. Some bosses could handle poor job performance and gave second chances. Mr. Chang wasn't one of those bosses. He wasn't one for gentle correction through performance reviews or training. No, he was more inclined to feed a mouthy insubordinate to the sharks. Frazer supposed that ruthlessness was just part and parcel of running an international criminal enterprise. One's tolerance for mistakes and second guessing had to be necessarily thin. After all, Mr. Chang's name was atop the most wanted lists of the FBI, the DEA, and a whole alphabet soup of law enforcement organizations. If he'd managed to evade capture for all these years, it was because his methods worked.

Frazer shrugged. "Of course. You're right, as always."

"See that you remember that." Mr. Chang gave him a look that made his blood run cold. "Now, if you don't mind, I'd like to get on with this delivery."

Frazer moved aside, making sure to stay out of the way of the helicopter's whirring rotors. It may have been a small remote controlled aircraft, but it was no child's toy. He leaned against the side of the boat and watched his boss pilot the miniature helicopter on a course for Molokai, where it would make delivery of several million dollars' worth of precious cargo. Frazer wondered what Mr. Chang would do if an errant seabird flew into the rotors and brought the helicopter crashing down into the ocean. He dismissed the thought. It was above his paygrade.

Donna and Taryn made sure the newlyweds were set up at their beach campsite then headed back to the landing strip. Theirs was schedule with plenty of wiggle room, and they took it easy, following the scenic path like a couple of tourists, even though it added a half hour to the trip. It wasn't the most direct route, but it was more of pleasant stroll than a hike. The path zigzagged through a lush forest to the top of a hill that over-looked the beach. Donna set a fast pace, but Taryn didn't mind. All those early morning workouts were paying off. She wasn't the least bit winded when they emerged from the trees onto the dirt road. A hundred yards ahead, the road forked. Heading west would take you to the Daioo family's estate, while going east would take you back to the landing strip. From there, it was a short hop back to their house on the opposite side of the island or a slightly longer trip back to Molokai Cargo HQ.

Taryn didn't know if the day's itinerary would take them back to the warehouse or if they planned to keep the plane overnight after delivering the snake to the wildlife center. She left those sorts of details up to Donna. After all, she was the hotshot agent, and Taryn was just along for the ride as long as she needed to be in the witness protection program. Which, if Taryn was being honest with herself, was probably the rest of her life. The mob had a notoriously long memory. It was sort of a bummer to think about it in those terms, but she supposed it could have been worse. She didn't have any family to leave behind. She was an only child and her parents had both been dead for years. There was no painful severing of ties. And there sure as hell were worse places to wind up. Even though Molokai wasn't exactly a buzzing hub of entertainment, it was still Hawaii, and who could complain about that? And as far as roommates went, Donna wasn't bad. A little serious maybe, but who could blame her? Life in the Agency wasn't exactly a laugh riot.

"So, how was your time with Rowdy?" Taryn asked as they paused to take in the view at the top of the hill. "And don't even try to tell me that your relationship is strictly professional."

"It was nice," Donna said. "Rowdy is…"

"He's a stud," Taryn finished for her. "Come on, Miss Badass Agent, just admit that you spent two weeks in Malibu getting your mind blown by that sexy cowboy while I was stuck all alone with no one but my battery powered boyfriend and my VHS collection to keep me company."

Donna started walking. She called back over her shoulder, "I don't kiss and tell. Now come on, let's get back to the plane. The sooner we get this snake delivered, the sooner we can jump in the Jacuzzi."

"Okay, but don't think I'm letting you off the hook," Taryn said as she trotted to catch up. "I want all the juicy details. If I can't have a sex life of my own, I can at least live vicariously through yours."

"If that's the best you can do, I'm sorry that like on Molokai is so boring. Maybe we should spend more time in town. There's bound to be someone that's boyfriend material there." Donna grabbed her arm and pulled her to a halt. She cocked her head to one side and asked, "Do you hear that?"

"What? I don't…"

But then Taryn heard it. A faint but growing buzz that was just audible over the dull roar of the surf. It sounded mechanical.

"Look!" Donna pointed overhead.

"A helicopter?" Taryn shaded her eyes against the sun. "That's weird. It's so small."

"And it's landing," Donna said. "Come on, let's go check it out."

They took the west road, following the helicopter—which Taryn figured was either remote controlled or piloted by squirrels—in the direction of the Daioo estate. Taryn knew that the Daioo family ran a small marijuana farm. Donna had told her that the Agency gave the family a pass in exchange for information about the bigger players in the drug trafficking game. The helicopter was probably just a rich kid's toy. Herman Daioo's grandsons had probably sampled a bit of the family's wares and decided to take the remote controlled helicopter for a spin. Probably harmless, but it would have been a waste of breath to suggest Donna let it go.

"Check it out." Donna pointed to a spot in a clearing a hundred yards ahead. "It's going to land right there."

Taryn slowed her pace just a bit and looked overhead. Sure enough, the helicopter was descending.

Good, she thought. The sooner Donna could satisfy her curiosity, the sooner they could get back home and into the Jacuzzi, maybe open a couple wine coolers. After a couple drinks, Donna is sure to dish out all the juicy details about Rowdy.

Up close, the helicopter was even smaller than Taryn had thought. From nose to tail, it wasn't more than three feet long. But if it was a toy, it was a damn expensive one. It was solidly built and appeared to be crammed full of electronic equipment.

Donna squatted next to the helicopter. "Well, this is interesting. It looks like this thing is carrying cargo."

Taryn shrugged off her backpack and dropped to one knee and got a look for herself. One of the small cockpit doors swung open automatically, revealing that cargo that Donna was talking about: two small metal boxes. They reminded Taryn of her ex-husband's cigarette case. She grabbed them out of the helicopter and held them up for inspection.

"Doesn't feel like there's much in here," she said. "Small cargo, whatever it is."

"You should be careful," Donna warned. "Those could be explosives."

"Oh, yeah, like that would make total sense." Taryn rolled her eyes. She loved Donna, but sometimes the girl could be so damn serious.

"Even James Bond exercises some caution," Donna said.

"Give me a break. This island is too boring for 007."

The words had barely passed her lips when the shouting started. Two men were coming down the road, and they didn't appear pleased to see the women.

"Hey!" one of the men shouted. "Get the hell away from there!"

"Yeah," the other added. "That's our fucking helicopter!"

That struck Taryn as strange. Maybe she was vain, but in her experience, most men were

happy to see a pair of blonde babes taking an interest in their hobby. And these two especially didn't look like they were in any position to be picky. They weren't exactly going to be mistaken for Calvin Klein models. One of them had a ridiculous horseshoe mustache and straw colored hair that looked like it had been trimmed by a barber on acid. His partner was a hefty Islander with a patchy beard and a single dangly earring. Their outfits looked like they came off the rack at some tourist trap discount store. Not exactly classy dudes. But it wasn't their fashion sense that worried Taryn. She was more concerned with the fact that both of them were armed with sawed-off double barrel shotguns. Those certainly didn't come from a tourist trap discount store.

"Better get ready to put some of that martial arts training to use," Donna said.

Taryn slipped the two metal cases into her pocket. She

unzipped her backpack and groped blindly through its contents. Mostly, it was the usual boring stuff: a bottle of water, some granola bars, a first aid kit, and a map of the island. But beneath all that boring stuff was a pair of wooden nunchakus. Taryn had chosen this particular weapon because she'd liked watching Bruce Lee twirl them around in some movie. For the last few months, Donna had been putting her through the paces with martial arts training. Taryn had mostly just thought it was a fun way of keeping in shape. More fun that step aerobics anyway. But now, it looked like she might have to put that training to the test.

"Stop right there!" Donna shouted. Her tone was all business, but it didn't slow the men one bit.

"I don't think they plan on stopping," Taryn said as she slid the nunchakus from the backpack.

Donna shook her head slowly. Her fingers dipped into her boot and unsnapped the ankle holster within. She pulled out a pair of ninja throwing stars, which Donna insisted on calling *shiruken*, their points honed to a wicked edge that glinted in the tropical sunlight.

"Freeze!" Mr. Horseshoe mustache shouted, firing a blast from his shotgun.

The shot wounded a nearby tree. Either he was a terrible marksman or it was intended as a warning shot, Taryn figured. Either way, it was all the invitation she and Donna needed to get to work.

Donna flung one of her stars at the big guy. The blades caught him in the shoulder, eliciting a scream that was so girlish Taryn might have found it funny under different circumstances. Instead of laughing, she ran forward and dealt Mr. Mustache a vicious body blow with her nunchakus. He made a choking sound as he struggled to raise his shotgun. Taryn didn't give him a chance. She dropped back one step and swung the nunchakus into his crotch. This time, he didn't just make a gagging sound. He doubled over and vomited into the grass. Taryn brought her knee up into his face, crunching his nose. He staggered, hunched over, but managed to keep his balance and his gun.

She glanced over her shoulder just as Donna flipped her remaining star at the big man. For a man of his size—and one who was already wounded—he stepped lightly, dodging out of the star's trajectory. Taryn ran to her friend's aid, but Donna grabbed her arm and tugged her away.

"Let's get out of here," she said. "These guys might have backup on the way, and we can't afford to blow our cover any worse than it's already blown."

As Taryn broke into a run, she felt one of the metal boxes drop out of her pocket. She skidded to a halt, casting her gaze around in the tall grass to find it. But by then, Mr. Mustache had recovered enough to send another shotgun blast their way.

"Forget it!" Donna insisted. "You still got the other one. Now, let's get to the plane before those guys can reload."

Harry screamed as he pulled the throwing star from his shoulder. Blood soaked through his floral-print shirt, staining the pink hibiscus blooms dark red. His partner, Mike, huffed and puffed as he drew up alongside him. His hand was thrust into his pants and he winced with each step.

"She whacked me in the balls, man," he gasped. "I think she broke one of them."

"Yeah, well, I got cut up by one of them ninja stars," Harry said. "Can you believe that? Like something out of a kung-fu movie. Who the hell were those broads?"

"Whoever they were, they're long gone now," Mike replied, pointing skyward as a Cessna began its ascent into the clouds. "Guess they're not just ninjas, but pilots too. But never

mind that. Let's get the stuff and head into town. Not a good idea to keep Seth waiting."

They limped across the clearing to where the remote control helicopter had set down. Harry wondered if he was going to require stitches. The idea made him nauseous. He hated needles. But at least he didn't get his balls smashed in. Mike was wheezing and groaning like a man on the verge of death. When he crouched down next to the helicopter, he made a sound like halfway between a whimper and a cough. Then he pounded his fist on the ground.

"Damn it!" He pounded again. "There's nothing here. They took the boxes."

Harry was already queasy from thinking about needles, but the bottom of his stomach seemed to fall out at the sound of Mike's news.

"What do you mean?" Harry gasped.

"I mean there's nothing in this damn helicopter. Those broads took it." Mike rose unsteadily to his feet. "You know what it'll be like going to Seth empty-handed?"

Harry winced as he pressed a hand to his wounded shoulder. "Oh, man..."

Before Harry could answer, the helicopter's engine chugged to life. They stepped back, out of the range of the spinning rotors, and watched as the small aircraft rose from the ground. It chugged off in the direction of the beach, eventually disappearing over the horizon.

It was Donna's idea to head back to their house instead of delivering the snake to the wildlife institute. Taryn wasn't sure what rattled her more, the attack they'd just survived or the fact that Donna seemed so shaken up by it. Until now, Taryn had always viewed Donna as fearless and indomitable, a blonde Valkyrie in khaki cut-offs. Then again, this was the first time that Taryn had seen her in full-on combat mode. All things considered, Donna seemed to be taking it in stride, and Taryn did her best to calm her own nerves.

Landing the Cessna in the driveway was far from ideal. With such a short landing strip, it was a difficult task that required nerves of steel and lightning reflexes. Fortunately, Donna possessed both, and she put them down with room to spare.

"What about the snake?" Taryn asked as the plane came to a stop just a few yards shy of the Jeep.

Donna killed the engine and tugged the headset off her ears. "Damn, I hadn't thought of that. You think it will be okay?"

Taryn smiled. Finally, she got to be the expert on something. It was a rare opportunity to impress her roommate, and she seized it eagerly.

"Well, it just so happens I know a thing or two about snakes," she said, sliding out of the cockpit and motioning for Donna to follow her to the rear of the plane.

"Yeah, I just bet you know all there is to know about snake handling," Donna laughed.

Taryn rolled her eyes at the joke. She popped the door on the cargo hold and slapped the crate. "I'm not sure what species we got here exactly, but it appears to be a constrictor of some kind. They're carnivores and often eat animals larger than themselves. A lot of times, they crush their prey and swallow it whole. Like, they eat their prey while it's still alive. Pretty gross, huh?"

Donna gagged theatrically. "Gross is an understatement. How do you know all this stuff?"

"One of the guys my ex-husband worked with was named Gordy the Snake. Wanna guess how he intimidated people? I'll tell you: he'd make them watch his pet python eat." Taryn paused for dramatic effect, then continued, "Anyway, he liked to talk about his prize pet. He once told me that it could go two weeks between feedings. I figure this snake has been so sleepy because it was fed before they packed it in the crate. It should be fine in the garage."

"Good," Donna said. "Then let's put it in the garage, then go relax in the Jacuzzi for a minute. I can use some downtime after that ambush back there. And while we're at it, we can see what's in that box you took out of the little helicopter."

A few minutes later, the snake was safely stowed in the garage and the Jacuzzi was bubbling away. The two roommates, long past the need for modesty in each other's presence, shed their clothes. A dip in the hot tub always felt better when you were naked. Wisps of steam rose from the surface of the water. Donna climbed in with zero hesitation, but Taryn lowered herself into the water slowly. It was just one notch shy of being too hot, but it only took a moment to acclimate. Then, as she reclined, her muscles began to unknot. She sighed contentedly.

"After a day like we just had," Donna said, "there's no place like home."

"You got that right," Taryn replied, she stretched her arms over her head.

For a moment, they enjoyed the relaxing bath in silence, then Taryn asked again how Rosie's time with Rowdy had been. She pressed her for some hot details.

"Come on, Donna. You get to spend a couple weeks with a hunky guy who lives on a yacht, while I was back here by myself. It's been so long since I've had some male attention that I'm starting to wonder if I remember what it feels like."

It was the truth, sadly. Since her arrival in Molokai, Taryn had been as celibate as a nun. Well, apart from a one-time thing with an ex-football player, anyway. But one night stands didn't count. They were just enough to work up an appetite without truly satisfying it. She'd tried channeling her energy into other pursuits. At first, she'd entertained thoughts of becoming a surfer. That didn't last long. Getting pummeled by waves wasn't her idea of fun. Then she'd tried fishing. The idea of using a simple fishing rod and reel seemed boring, but spearfishing sounded mighty exciting. She'd never mastered the traditional version, so she'd purchased a spear gun. Turns out it's harder to aim at underwater targets than she'd expected. Now, the spear gun was collecting dust in the hall closet alongside her surfing gear. Maybe the next hobby, whatever it turned out to be, would actually suit her.

"You're not going to tell me one single detail, are you?" Taryn asked, playfully splashing a bit of water at her roommate.

Donna just smiled.

"All right, be that way." Taryn blew a lock of hair out of her eyes. "Hey, why don't you see what's in that box I picked up earlier?"

Donna turned aside to grab her set of lock picks from the edge of the tub. Then she grabbed the small box from the helicopter and got to work.

"You think you can get it open?" Taryn asked.

Donna laughed. "Girl, you should know better than to ask that."

A few twists of the thin metal tools and a series of muttered curses was all it took for her to pop the lock. She flipped open the lid and spilled the contents into her palm, holding them up for Taryn's inspection.

"Diamonds!" Taryn gasped, sloshing across the tub to get a closer look. "Big ones, too. These must be worth a fortune. No wonder they tried to kill us."

"Yeah, and that's why we're in some big trouble."

"You think they know who we are?" Taryn counted a dozen stones, each of them the size of a fingertip. She was no expert, but she knew how much her best earrings had cost, and the diamonds in those weren't even half the size of these. Hell, they weren't a tenth of the size.

"Taryn, how many women fly around this island in a cargo plane?" Donna asked.

"Just one, Kemosabe. I'm getting out of here," Taryn said.

"Yeah? And where do you think you'll go where there's not a price on your head? Like it or not, you're stuck here with me."

Taryn slumped down in the water. "Okay, so what's the plan?"

"First step is to report to Rowdy. He's the agent in charge of the division."

"Yeah, but before you make that call, you better call the wildlife park people and have them pick up that snake. The sooner we get that thing out the house, the better."

Edy circulated through the dining room with ease and grace, gliding from one table to another as she greeted the customers. There was the usual mixture of locals and tourists, distinguishable by the degree to which they were sunburned. Even after the lunch rush had mostly died down, the room was still crowded. The soundtrack of piped-in exotica jazz mingled with the buzz of conversation and bursts of laughter. It was, Edy decided, another fine day in paradise.

Edy's Bar and Grill was a semi-fashionable spot that was the hub of Molokai's night life. A short walk from the east side beach, it had opened as The Hula Hut in the months following statehood and had operated under various names since then. The current owner was the establishment's namesake, Edy St. James, a former Miss America runner up and toothpaste spokesmodel from the mainland. Under her management, the place had thrived with locals and tourists alike, a rare feat for any bar or restaurant on the small island. Edy herself was a big part of the bar's success. She was a hands-on manager who was seemingly always present. The same smile that had made her such a hit with the toothpaste executives endeared her to the customers and employees. It was hard to be in a bad mood for long with that thousand-watt smile shining at you.

The doorman/host, on the other hand, wasn't so well-liked. He was a slick, wannabe Don Juan named Ashley McBride. Edy didn't care for him or his eye-wateringly strong aftershave, but his father had invested heavily in the business, so she was obliged to keep him on, despite her distaste.

Currently, Ashley was involved in some banter with Charlotte O'Daniel, an ex-swimsuit model who was one of the bar's regulars. As Edy neared the front of the room, she caught some of Ashley's groan-inducing lines.

"You know, Charlotte baby, I haven't seen you in a while," Ashley said, whipping a comb through his overly styled hair. "Where you been?"

"I'm just a working girl," Charlotte replied. "I can't afford to eat in this joint every day."

Edy knew times had been tough for Charlotte since she lost her contract as a Coppertone model, but she suspected that her recent absence had more to do with Ashley's heavy-handed approach than any financial woes. After all, there was no shortage of men willing to buy a woman like Charlotte a Mai Tai and a poke bowl. Hell, there was no shortage of men willing to propose marriage on the spot. Edy knew that routine. Most of them were dirty old men, recently divorced and looking to impress their pot-bellied friends with some arm candy. Some women were built for that, but Edy certainly wasn't, and she suspected Charlotte was similar in that regard.

"Baby, you can eat my joint anytime," Ashley oozed. "For free. All the meat you want."

"That makes me want to turn into a vegetarian."

Edy took that as her cue to rescue the poor girl. She told Ashley to get back to work on the reservation book, then led Charlotte across the dining room to where her date was eagerly awaiting her. The date in question was an aging TV exec named Whitey Andrews. If he'd been a regular joe, Charlotte would have been so far out of his league she might as well have been in another galaxy. But Whitey had ties to a major network and Charlotte was out of a job. Edy felt bad for the girl, but that was how the world worked, even in paradise. You used what you had to get ahead. And what Charlotte had were on full display in a low-cut blouse and push-up bra. Whitey couldn't have maintained eye contact with her for more than a few seconds, not even if he had a gun pointed at his head.

Charlotte had barely gotten settled in her chair before Whitey launched into a monologue about the depths of his affection for her. Edy excused herself, but she hovered within earshot. The scene at the table had all the makings of good drama. Edy wasn't proud of eavesdropping, but she took her entertainment where she could get it.

"I'm not just some fast talking New York TV executive," Whitey said. "I really care about you, Charlotte. I really do…"

"Really?" Charlotte sniffed. "You practically raped me last night."

Whitey didn't miss a beat. "That was last night, baby. Today, I really care about you. And not just your body, either. I care about your mind."

"Oh yeah? Well, I'll tell you right now, there's certain things I won't do, no matter how much I need a job."

Whitey took a breath, preparing to further plead his case, but a passing waitress caught his eye. The waitresses at Edy's Bar and Grill enjoyed a lax dress code, and this particular waitress, a twenty-one year old beach bunny named Gina, took full advantage of that policy. She wore a short skirt and a pair of high heels, while considerable endowments were held in check by a string bikini top.

"Come on, Charlotte," Whitey said, his eyes still firmly fixed on Gina's twins. "Let's order a pair of coffee and talk it over. A *cup* of coffee, I mean…"

Edy walked away before it became impossible for her to contain her laughter. Her slow circuit of the room ended at Seth Romero's table. He was, as usual, dressed to the nines in a white suit with a silk shirt and tie. His hair was slicked back from his forehead, glistening with expensive pomade. An athletic blonde with iceberg blue eyes sat at his left, looking thoroughly bored as she picked at a salad. She looked like she'd rather be at the gym, bench pressing a couple tons.

"Everything okay, Mr. Romero?" Edy asked.

"Of course, Edy," Romero flashed her a smile. It was like being greeted by a shark. "The food is delicious."

"Let me know if you need anything," she said.

There were plenty of stories about Seth Romero going around, and none of them were the type that inspired warm, fuzzy feelings. The way Edy had heard it, his mother had been a female KGB agent who'd been sent to Cuba before the missile crisis. While she was on the island, she'd shacked up with one of Castro's trigger men. That unholy union had spawned Seth Romero, who, at the tender age of twenty-six, had become the most feared player in Hawaii's drug trade. He was a regular diner at Edy's Bar and Grill, dropping in two or three times a week for a rare steak and a shrimp cocktail. In his own words, he preferred the relative quiet of Molokai to the hustle and bustle of Honolulu. When he wined and dined one of his criminal associates, he did so at Edy's. And for that reason, Edy was regularly in contact with any number of federal agencies looking to lock up Romero and those in his orbit. She watched and she listened, that was all. No wearing a wire, no heavy eavesdropping. All in all, it was any easy gig.

At first, Edy had started collecting info as a way of working off a debt. She'd been picked up for DWI in Maui, doing ninety in a Alfa Romeo Spider she'd "borrowed" from a boyfriend. During the search of the vehicle, the cops had found a half-ounce of marijuana and a baggie of pills that turned out to be Quaaludes. In exchange for her cooperation, Edy had been let off with a warning. A few years later, after her debt to the government had long been paid, Edy still did some eavesdropping for the feds voluntarily. A true story of reform and redemption, she liked to think.

Edy excused herself and headed for the front of the dining

room, where Ashley was trying to slime his way into the panties of some sunburnt beach bunny with a German accent.

"Well, *fraulein*, how would you like to sample some local bratwurst?" he asked. "I'm sure you'll find it even more satisfying than what you could get back home."

The German tourist giggled. Edy rolled her eyes and sighed inwardly.

Seth Romero wasn't known for being slow to anger. And that's why he went from zero to sixty at the first sight of his two top watchdogs, Harry and Mike, making their way onto the patio of Edy's Bar and Grill. Seth believed wholeheartedly in the old adage about good help being hard to find. In his experience, it was doubly true for an entrepreneur of the criminal underworld, such as himself. Harry and Mike were as close as had to reliable employees for everyday grunt work, and that was pretty damn sad. You'd think a place like Hawaii would have better talent on hand, either homegrown or of the imported variety.

"Goddamn it, they had one simple job," he said, wiping his mouth and tossing the napkin onto the table. He looked at Rosie and said, "Excuse me for a moment, dear."

Rosie nodded and continued poking her fork at her salad but not actually eating anything.

Seth's heartbeat was already thudding away like a bass drum before his two employees could even get a word out. He maneuvered them into a corner of the patio and demanded that they explain themselves.

"You better have a damn good reason for showing up here," he said.

No one would ever mistake Mike Neville for a genius, but compared to Harry Kapua, he was a bona fide MENSA candidate. And that's probably why he spoke up first.

"Now calm down, Mr. Romero," Mike said. "We've got some bad news."

"Don't tell me to calm down," Seth snapped. "I'm the boss and I'll act however I want, understand? I gave you one simple task: pick up my merchandise and take it back to the house. And yet here you are, interrupting my lunch. Explain yourselves."

Harry decided it was his turn to add to the discussion. "Somebody beat us to the stuff. They got away."

"It looks like they almost killed you," Seth said, looking his men over.

Harry's shoulder was heavily bandaged, and Mike's nose looked like he'd gone a couple rounds with Mike Tyson. He still had dried blood in that stupid mustache of his.

"Well, don't keep me in suspense," Seth growled. "Who were these men that kicked your asses? I guess they must have been some real bad dudes if they got the drop on you, right?"

Harry and Mike exchanged a glance. Then Harry took a deep breath and winced as he admitted the truth.

"It was a couple broads," he said.

"Broads?" Seth thought he might blow a gasket right there and then. "You fucking dummies. You let a couple broads get away with my merchandise?"

"We didn't expect them to come at us with fucking ninja weapons," Mike whined. "The had those things, you know, *numb chucks*, and those throwing stars. I'm telling you, these broads were like trained assassins or something. And then they got away on a cargo plane. It said 'Molokai Cargo' on the side."

"Trained ninja assassins? A Molokai Cargo plane?" Seth sniffed. "If brains were bird shit, you two would have a clean cage. I'll get someone else to handle them. Now get out of here before I decide to do some damage you won't walk away from."

They may have been idiots, but Harry and Mike had enough brains to get the hell out of there. Seth stood on the patio for a moment, watching them beat a retreat to the parking lot, then he went back inside and sat down at his table. There was still a half-eaten New York strip on his plate, but he'd lost his appetite.

"Well?" Rosie asked, sipping from her glass of white wine.

Seth gave her a slow appraisal. Rosie was just as deadly as she was beautiful. If someone was comfortable jacking his merchandise in broad daylight, it might be time to utilize Rosie's talents.

"I think I've got a job for you," Seth said.

Chapter Five

Rowdy Abilene feinted with a quick right jab, then attempted a leg sweep. Jade saw right through the feint and sidestepped the leg sweep like it was nothing. Hell, the guy might as well have yawned. Sometimes, sparring with him could be downright humiliating.

"Come on," Jade chuckled. "Your hips give you away every time. Gotta bend like a reed in the wind, remember?"

Rowdy tried another combination, but Jade wasn't having it. This time, he actually did yawn.

"As your karate instructor," Jade said, "as well as your friend, I'm not going to take it easy on you."

Rowdy bounced back and squared his shoulders just in time for Jade to aim a spinning heel kick right at his face. Jade's foot stopped less than inch shy of Rowdy's jaw.

"Gotcha," Jade said.

"Is that right? Maybe I just let you win because I felt sorry for you." Rowdy raised his fists. "You see these hands? They're lethal weapons, my friend."

"Confucius say man with deadly hands must be careful when slapping on aftershave." Jade mimed a slap to his own face.

"Yeah or when choking the chicken, right?"

Jade threw back his head and laughed. The guy might have been a karate master and an agent with an impressive service record, but his sense of humor had yet to graduate junior high. As far as partners went, Rowdy couldn't have asked for better. Yeah, it took a little getting used to the fact that Jade had only one name—like Prince or Madonna or Cher—but Rowdy could let that slide. The guy was a rock solid investigator and there wasn't a man in the agency Rowdy would rather have at his side when the going got tough.

They'd spent the morning sparring on the deck of Rowdy's yacht. All things considered, Rowdy would have preferred sparring with Donna. Her methods were just as vigorous, but far more pleasant. Had it really only been a couple days since she'd left the mainland? Rowdy sighed. It wasn't like him to get so hung up on a chick. He felt like he was somehow disgracing the family name. After all, the Abilenes were known far and wide as ladies' men. Why, just think of what his cousin Cody would say if he heard that Rowdy had fallen in love?

"Head out of the clouds, buddy," Jade said, grabbing a towel from the stack on a nearby deck chair. "The sushi man is on his way. Hope he's got good news today."

Rowdy followed Jade's line of sight to the far side of the marina. A chubby man on a small dirt bike was approaching at a speed that could have been considered reckless for a rider not quite as experienced as Bob Kwan.

"Man, look at Bob dodge through those people," Rowdy marveled. "Dude has catlike reflexes, huh?"

"Yeah," Jade agreed. "I wonder if he telegraphs his leg sweeps too?"

"Don't make me angry, man. You wouldn't like me when I'm angry."

Bob gunned the dirt bike's engine as he headed down the slip where the *Malibu Express* was moored. He brought the bike to screeching halt, then dismounted and retrieved a Styrofoam to-go box from the saddle bag.

"Here's some early lunch, fellas," he said, passing the box to Rowdy.

"Yummy." Rowdy held the box to his nose and sniffed. "But no tip for delivery this time,

Bob. I'll have to get you on your next visit. You know I'm good for it."

"Yeah, right, you cheap motherfucker." Bob shot him the middle finger, but smiled. As far as agency couriers went, Bob was the best. And it was a nice touch that he delivered messages with actual food.

"Take it easy, fellas," Bob said. "I'll catch you next time."

He jumped back on his dirt bike and kicked it into gear. The tourists strolling the marina scattered at his approach.

"Looks like some tuna rolls and spicy dumplings," Rowdy said, popping the lid on the box. "Oh, and what's this? A message from HQ! Imagine my shock and surprise."

Jade reached across him and plucked a folded scrap of paper from beneath a single-serving pouch of wasabi. He unfolded the message and read it.

"Let me guess," Rowdy said. "We got trouble in paradise."

"Bad juju over on Molokai, amigo. The bodies of those two missing cops just washed up on shore. Well, what was left of them, anyway. Guess we're going to be looking into that. And that means paying your girlfriend a visit. Lucky you." Jade pulled a cigarette lighter from his pocket and torched the message.

"I'm sure Edy will be there too," Rowdy said. "Guess I'm not the only lucky one."

"We ride at dawn, poncho!" Jade grabbed a dumpling. "But first, let's eat. Kicking your ass always works up an appetite."

"Well, well, well," Donna said, following Taryn into her bedroom. "It looks like someone did some redecorating while I was in Malibu."

Taryn shrugged. "Hey, I got bored."

"It looks like the lobby of a movie theater in here," Donna said, looking over the selection of movie posters plastered to the walls.

Taryn slipped out of her bathrobe and grabbed a tank top and shorts from her dresser. Donna was similarly attired in a pair of men's boxer shorts and a faded grey t-shirt. They were in for the night, so there wasn't any point in getting dressed up.

"Hey, you got a *Malibu Express* poster!" Donna said. "And right above your bed? Girl, get a grip."

"Hey, the video store threw it in for free. It's hard for a girl to get her kicks in a place like this, but I do what I can." Taryn pulled her hair into a messy ponytail. "And besides, Cody Abilene is a total babe."

"Yeah, it's too bad we don't hear from him much these days. Not since he left the agency to become an actor."

Donna still thought that whole situation was like something out of a bad B-movie. A hotshot private detective solves a case involving blackmail, murder, and espionage, then gets recruited to the agency, where he quickly becomes a decorated field operative. And then, as if that wasn't enough, he gets cast as the lead in a movie based on that career-making espionage case. From private dick to secret agent to Hollywood hunk…it was a hell of a story.

"Rowdy and Cody are cousins, right?" Taryn asked.

"Yeah, and they're both adorable, but just a little bit flaky, you know?" Donna replied.

"So tell me the truth about Rowdy. How's his, you know, *stuff?*"

Donna shrugged. "It's great. Four, maybe four and a half inches."

"Girl, you gotta get out more if you think that's great," Taryn laughed.

"Well, I was measuring from the ground up…"

Taryn rolled her eyes. She grabbed the box of diamonds off the top of her dresser. "Hey, I'm going to put this ice in the freezer. Why don't you order us a pizza? After the day we had, I think we deserve pepperoni with extra cheese, and maybe we can watch Malibu Express, so you can catch up with Cody Abilene."

Donna dropped onto the bed and grabbed the phone from the nightstand. "Bring me a can of Tab while you're at it."

"You got it." Taryn padded out of the room.

Donna put the receiver to her ear, but there was no dial tone. That was all it took for her sixth sense to start sending out red alerts. She dropped the phone back onto its cradle and shouted, "Taryn, come on, let's get out of here!"

She sprang off the bed as the bedroom door burst open. A black-clad figure strode into the room. His face was obscured by a ski mask, and he held a knife in one hand.

"All right, bitch," he growled, grabbing a fistful of Donna's shirt. "Tell me where the diamonds are and maybe I won't gut you like a fish."

Donna brought up her knee, trying for a crotch shot, but the man dodged it. He slammed her into the wall.

"Listen," he growled. "You hear that? My partner has your roommate out there. One of you better start talking."

Donna could hear the sound of a struggle in the kitchen. Taryn was screaming curses, while another voice—a woman's voice, if Donna had to guess—barked orders in reply. Donna made a tactical decision. With both intruders within earshot, she and Taryn had little chance of escape. She needed to divide them. If Taryn could just hold up a little longer…

"Okay, okay," Donna said. "They're out back in the garage. There's a file cabinet…"

"Come on," the man snarled. "Show me."

He frog-marched Donna out of the bedroom and down the hall, towards the back door. So far, it was going exactly how Donna had hoped. Going through the front door would have taken them past the kitchen, where Taryn might have panicked at the sight of Donna being held at knife-point.

Donna stepped out of the back door, wincing as her bare feet came down on the oyster shell path. She did her best to appear terrified and compliant as she ran through the various close combat scenarios. Her agency training had been intense, and it was going to take more than some low-level thug with a knife to frighten her into submission. She just needed an opening, then she could fight her way through this asshole and get back to the house. She reminded herself that while Taryn may have looked like a princess type, the girl had faced down two mob hitmen without flinching. All she needed to do was stall the other intruder for another minute, maybe two.

The thug shoved Donna into the garage and flipped the light switch just inside the doorway. There was only one light in the garage—a single bulb ceiling fixture—and it did little to cut the darkness. That was another reason Donna had steered him out here. Fighting would be that much more difficult in the cluttered, shadowy interior, especially for someone unfamiliar with the room's layout.

She led her captor across the room, past the work bench atop which rested the wooden crate containing the snake. Donna caught a glimpse of a forked tongued darting out from between the crate's slats. The snake let out an evil-sounding hiss as they passed. If the thug noticed, he didn't say anything.

"Okay, don't move." The thug shoved Donna against the wall next to the filing cabinet.

He tugged open the top drawer and began rifling through the contents.

"No, it's in the middle drawer," Donna said. She drew in a slow, steady breath, preparing herself.

"It better be in here. I'm not playing games with you…"

As the thug bent to open the lower drawer, Donna made her move. She grabbed him by the back of his ski mask and slammed his head into the metal filing cabinet. He recovered quickly, swiping at her with his knife. But the move had taken him off balance, and Donna landed a kick to his stomach. He reeled backwards into the work bench. The snake's crate wobbled then fell. The impact snapped two of the crate's slats, leaving just enough room for the snake to slither through.

The thug screamed at the sight of the immense specimen. For such a muscly tough guy, he sure did panic easy. He danced back on tiptoe like some cartoon housewife frightened by the sight of a mouse. He tripped on a cardboard box full of Christmas decorations and went down hard. It was actually pretty funny, like real life slapstick, but Donna didn't hang around to laugh. After all, he was still holding a knife, while she was unarmed. And Taryn was still inside the house.

Donna picked her way through the clutter and stepped out of the garage into the cool night air. She'd almost made it to the house's back door when she heard the gunshots.

Taryn didn't like having her own weapon of choice—the nunchakus—used against her. It felt like an insult. But the woman wielding was too tall and powerfully built for Taryn to even consider her options for fighting back. If only she was farther along in her martial arts training, maybe she could have tried something. Now, the best she could do was try not to get herself

killed and hope like hell Donna was on the way.

The woman shoved her against the refrigerator and stepped back, swinging the nunchakus in front of her with such force that Taryn could feel the air whooshing by her face.

"Where are the diamonds?" the woman demanded. "Tell me

and I won't be forced to bust you up. It'd be a shame to spoil that pretty face…"

To drive the point home, the woman swung the nunchakus at the counter, reducing a coffee mug to ceramic shards.

Taryn shook her head.

Another swing of the nunchakus shattered the cookie jar. Jagged bits of crockery and Oreos flew through the air like shrapnel. Taryn winced as the bits rained down around her. Another swing of the ninja weapon reduced set of salt and pepper shakers to bits. A third dented the refrigerator door.

"The next one is aimed at your face," the woman said.

"Okay, okay!" Taryn raised her hands in surrender. "They're in the freezer."

The woman yanked Taryn away from the refrigerator and shoved her to the floor. She opened the freezer and pulled out the small metal case.

"Okay, sweetheart, where's the other one?" she said, looming over Taryn.

"I don't have it…" Taryn wracked her brain, struggling to recall anything from her martial arts training that might help her.

Then the gunshots started. Taryn had heard of being saved by the bell, but being saved by a burst of gunfire was something new. The woman glanced from Taryn to the front door then back at Taryn. She cocked her head to one side, like a dog considering which corner of the yard to piss in.

"This isn't over, bitch," the woman said, thrusting the nunchakus into Taryn's face. "We want that other box of diamonds. We'll be back."

Before Taryn could offer anything in the way of a retort, the woman vaulted over her and ran out the front door.

This should have been a simple matter. Go in, shake those blonde broads down, get the diamonds, and go. Easy-peasy. Those bitches may have gotten the drop on Mike and Harry, but Rosie and her twin brother Kimo were another matter. When it came to busting heads, there wasn't a better brother-sister combo.

Seth had figured he'd just wait out front and have a cigarette while they went into the house and retrieved the merchandise. He leaned against the car and fired up a Camel Light while he watched Rosie and Kimo pick the lock on the front door. This whole thing was a headache, but it would be over soon and he could get back to business as usual. One thing was for sure: he was going to give Rosie the business like she'd never had before. All this frustration needed a release, to say nothing of the fact that the thought of her slapping those two broads around really stoked his engine. He wished they'd brought two cars. Then he wouldn't have to wait until they dropped Kimo at his place before getting down to it. The only thing was, Seth hoped the car ride to Kimo's place didn't kill the urge. Fucking a woman with an identical male twin could be disconcerting, especially because it didn't totally disgust Seth. Looking at Kimo, especially after a few drinks, could give Seth some confusing feelings. He was sure a shrink could have a field day with that information. Good thing Seth hadn't retained another shrink since he had to kill the last one for suggesting nasty stuff about Seth's mother...

Seth finished his cigarette. He dropped the butt and ground it under the heel of his Italian loafer.

Goddamn it, what's taking so long? he wondered.

He slipped another cigarette out of his monogrammed gold case and stuck it in his lips. He snapped his matching gold lighter and raised it to the cigarette's tip. In the flickering light of the flame, he saw the snake slither around the corner of the house. It paused and regarded him with its black, expression-less eyes.

"What the fuck?" The cigarette fell from Seth's lips.

It took a few seconds for his brain to adequately process the messages relayed by his senses, but one that information really sank in, Seth felt his stomach clench like a fist. He hated snakes. He really hated them. In fact, "hate" was too mild of a word to encompass the breadth of his disgust, repulsion, and loathing. In his estimation, snakes were the vilest creatures on earth, even worse than the winged cockroaches that had swarmed his child-hood home in Florida.

This particular snake was one of the vilest specimens he'd ever seen. Its hide was irregularly patterned, as if nature had assembled it from scraps left over from other snakes. Its head seemed somehow misshapen, but Seth couldn't put his finger on what gave him that impression. One thing was for sure, it was a big motherfucker, twenty feet long at least.

"You are one ugly son of a bitch." Seth's throat was suddenly dry, and his voice was reduced to a hoarse whisper. His upper lip curled in disgust as he raised his gun and fired.

The bullets impacted on the driveway, raising clouds of dust and oyster shell shrapnel. The snake appeared unbothered. It uncoiled to its full length and slithered along the house's foun-dation, its slimy forked tongue flicking in and out of its mouth as it went. Seth gagged in disgust, but managed to squeeze off shot after shot until the hammer clicked on an empty chamber.

The front door of the house burst open, and his two black-clad assassins ran toward him. The twin killers looked this way and that, attempting to locate the target of Seth's gunfire.

"We got the diamonds," Rosie said, holding aloft the small metal box. "Well, we got half of them anyway."

Seth only took his eyes off the snake for a moment, but that was long enough for the vile thing to disappear into the shad-ows. The plaintive song of police sirens struck up a chorus in the distance. He knew it was only a matter of minutes until the place was swarmed with cops. And while the local PD was the very definition of pathetic and ineffectual, Seth couldn't afford any legal entanglements, especially during this period of expansion.

"I can't believe what I just saw!" he shouted as his two employees reached the car. He tore the back door open. "Come on, let's get out of here!"

Kimo jumped into the driver's seat while Rosie sprinted around the car and took her place in the passenger seat. Seth scanned the night one more time, searching for the giant snake. If only he could get one more shot at it…

Had it not been for that snake, he would have been paying more attention and noticed the front door of the house swinging open to make way for the two blonde cargo pilots. By the time he saw that one of them was aiming a pistol at him, it was too late. Shrieking like an enraged wildcat, she snapped off a quick shot before he could even raise his own gun.

The bullet grazed Seth, ripping a bloody trench through his right cheek and taking off a bit of earlobe in the bargain.

"You son of a bitch!" the broad screamed, preparing to take another shot.

Seth didn't wait to see if her aim improved with the second shot. He dove into the backseat, his hand pressed to his wounded face. Kimo hit the gas, and the car sped into the night.

Donna's hand trembled as she lowered her gun. She stood there for a moment, catching her breath as she watched the retreating car's headlights disappear into the darkness. No matter how many times she'd drawn and fired her weapon in the line of duty—frankly, she'd lost count by this point—the come-down from the adrenaline burst always left her with butterflies in her stomach. She took a deep breath and let the tremors subside.

Taryn slipped an arm around her shoulders. "You okay, partner?"

"Yeah," Donna said. "Guess I sort of lost it there for a minute."

"No, you were great." Taryn gave her a brief squeeze before withdrawing her arm.

"That was Seth Romero, one of the meanest sons of bitches ever to set foot on the island," Donna sighed. "And I just blew a hole in his face. Not to mention I managed to set that snake free while I was wrestling that bastard who broke into the house."

"I guess it could be worse," Taryn said. "But all the same, I guess we better give Mr. Dickson a call and let him know what happened."

"Yeah. Those researchers at the wildlife park are going to be plenty disappointed." Donna shook her head. "Well, guess we better use the radio in the plane. One of those assholes cut the phone line before they broke in."

They made their way to the back of the house, where the Cessna was parked. Donna opened the pilot-side door and switched on the radio. In one of those rare moments of synchronicity in the universe, she was greeted by the static-choked voice of none other than Glen Dickson.

"This is HQ calling cargo plane November niner-niner-seven-eight-six…"

Donna thumbed the talkback button. "This is November niner-niner-seven-eight-six. Go ahead, Glen."

"I need you to listen carefully to everything I have to say…"

Donna got a bad feeling about what was coming. If Glen cut straight to the chase without any flirty preamble, something serious was up.

"We had a snake delivered from the Department of Health," Glen said. "It was bound for a government lab in Guam as part of some research project. I got a call from this guy in DC earlier today, and he gave me the lowdown on this thing. Let me tell you, this is no ordinary snake. It was grown in some military lab as a kind of biological weapon. It was raised on a diet of cancer-infected rats, and its venom carries a virulent strain of that disease. Not only that, but it has heightened levels of aggression. It will kill anything it comes across. You hear what I'm saying, Donna?"

"Yeah…" That bad feeling was starting to gain intensity.

"Now, my idiot nephews really screwed the pooch on this thing," Glen continued. "They mixed up this deadly mutant snake with the one that was meant for the wildlife park. You have the wrong snake. You hear me? You have the wrong snake!"

"No, we don't," Donna sighed.

"You're not understanding me, sweetheart. I'm telling you there was a mix-up…"

"And I'm telling you that we don't have any snake. It's a long story, but whatever snake we had got loose before we could make delivery."

"Then please, for the love of God, be careful. I'll get back to you, okay?"

"Roger that, boss. Over and out." Donna hung the radio back on its hook and turned to Taryn. "Guess you heard that, huh? What a day…"

"Let's get back inside," Taryn said. "That thing could be anywhere."

Donna let her roommate lead the way back into the house. The kitchen had been trashed during Taryn's struggle with the nunchaku-wielding intruder, so they set to work cleaning it up. One of the first items rescued from the floor was a photo of Donna's father. Donna picked it up and put it back in its usual spot, held to the refrigerator door with a magnet.

"You know," she said, running her fingertips over the photo, "he's still the most decorated operative in agency history. He dedicated himself to the pursuit of justice, and in the end, he gave his life for it. All I've ever wanted to do was follow in his footsteps."

Taryn grabbed the broom and started sweeping up the bits of shattered coffee mugs. "I'd say that you've achieved that goal."

"Really?" Donna shook her head. "Because tonight, I couldn't even handle two of Seth Romero's thugs. They nearly got both of us. To me, that feels like a betrayal of his memory."

A shaky sort of sadness stole over Donna. It had been a decade and change since her father had died while protecting a senator's daughter from a vengeful drug dealer, but she had yet to reconcile herself to his absence. He'd been her whole world. She'd never known her mother, who fell victim to a congenital heart defect only months after Donna was born. Her father was the only family she had.

"Hey," Taryn said, laying a comforting hand on Donna's shoulder. "I know he's looking down on you with nothing but pride in his heart. And don't forget, girl, you nearly put one in the head of the island's most ruthless drug lord. That bastard is lucky that I'm sweeping up busted coffee mugs instead of mopping his brains off the driveway. I mean, come on, you were just like James Bond out there."

Donna nodded, trying her best to convince herself that what Taryn said was true. "Yeah, but James Bond wouldn't have just grazed the guy. He'd have shot the bad guy then come in here and jump our bones."

"Yeah, but me first, of course," Taryn said.

The weight of the moment lifted, and they stood among the debris, laughing.

"I got an idea," Taryn continued once the giggles died down. "Let's leave the rest of this mess for tomorrow and head over to Edy's for a while. Our phone is out of order and we need to call Rowdy. Besides, I could use a drink."

"Well, I guess we do need to use the phone..."

"It'll be my treat," Taryn offered. "We can get dressed up and turn some heads while we're at it."

"Well," Donna said, "I guess a drink doesn't sound like a bad idea."

"That's the spirit! Now, I have this blouse you can borrow. It really puts the goodies on display, if you know what I mean."

Glen Dickson's indigestion was flaring up again. Sure, some of it was due to the massive amount of coffee he'd consumed during the last twelve hours, but he was convinced that most of it could be laid at the feet of his idiot nephews. This bullshit with the snake was going to be the death of his business, he just knew it. If not for the crates getting mixed up, he'd be home right now, sitting in his recliner with a cold beer in his hand while he watched whatever bullshit rerun was playing on the boob tube. Instead, he was sitting in his office, making phone calls to Washington DC in a desperate attempt to salvage something from this clusterfuck of mixed-up reptiles.

"What do you mean there's no Dr. Huang?" Glen asked, holding the phone between his ear and shoulder while he flipped through the day's cargo manifest. "I got it right here in front of me, in black and white. Says the snake was routed from a lab in Brazil. For some crazy reason, it made a stop in Hawaii on its way to your Guam office. The sender and recipient are both listed as a Dr. Huang."

"Sir, why would a specimen bound for our Guam office make a pit stop in Hawaii? That doesn't make sense, does it?" the health department secretary asked.

Glen pinched the bridge of his nose. As if the indigestion wasn't enough, he felt a migraine coming on. "Who knows? Probably a mistake. Not my fucking department. Boxes come in, boxes go out. That's all I know."

"And I know that there is not, and has never been, any Dr. Huang employed by this division. And our Guam office was closed two years ago during the last round of budget cuts. Everyone who worked there was reassigned, but none of them were named Huang." The secretary had that snippy tone of voice that set Glen's teeth on edge. "Now, will that be all?"

Glen hung up before he said something he'd end up regretting. He tore the sheet with all the info related to the snake off the clipboard and examined it one final time before feeding it into the document shredder. As far as he was concerned, that was the end of it. Unless Donna and Taryn managed to capture the snake, the whole business was over and done with. And he was more than happy to wash his hands of it. The more he looked into it, the more he got the idea that there was something shady about the shipment of the deadly snake. Hopefully, the goddamn thing would just slither into the brush and die.

He grabbed a roll of Tums from his desk drawer and thumbed a couple of the chalky white discs into his palm. He tossed them in his mouth and crunched them up. Once he'd gagged them down, he switched off his desk lamp and headed for the door. It was way past time to call it a day.

The snake slithered through the grass aimlessly. The largest prey it encountered were insects too small to bother ingesting. For a short while, it found amusement in savoring the exotic scents of its new environment, but it soon became bored. If no substantial prey was going to present itself, the snake decided to pursue its second favorite interest: sleeping. But to do so, it needed to find a suitable place to bed down.

Life in the jungle had taught the snake that sleeping in the open air was a dangerous proposition. As deadly as the snake was, its instinct told it that there was always something bigger and deadlier lurking just out of sight. So when it found a gap in the siding that covered the house's crawlspace, the snake forced itself through the opening, into the damp darkness. There, it set to work exploring the maze of pipes beneath the house. Intrigued by the sounds of running water, it examined each length of pipe until it came across an opening. The snake's desire to sleep was outweighed by its eagerness to explore further, and it slithered into the narrow confines of the pipe...

Chapter Six

Donna and Taryn were regulars at Edy's, so Ashley should have known better than to try one of his lines on them. But, Donna supposed, some guys just couldn't help themselves. Like a kid touching a hot stove, they insisted on learning lessons the hard way.

"Hey, ladies," he said, emerging from behind the front counter to greet them at the door. "Please, allow me to offer you the finest seat in the house."

Donna crossed her arms over her chest. "I know I'm going to regret asking, but where exactly is this so-called best seat?"

Ashley smiled. "Right here on my face."

"Oh, is that because your nose is bigger than your dick?" Donna shot back. Before he could recover enough to stammer out a reply, she asked if Edy was available.

"Yeah, yeah, sure thing," Ashley replied. He was flustered, but he shook it off enough to turn his thousand-watt smile back on full blast. "She's in the back, by the bar. Corner booth, you can't miss it."

Taryn leaned in to whisper a parting shot. "Don't worry, size isn't everything. You know, not the size of the boat but the motion in the ocean? At least that's what I've heard."

Donna rolled her eyes. "Don't encourage him."

They threaded their way through the maze of tables, past a table where two massive jocky types were polishing off enough food to serve a family of five. Just as Ashley promised, Edy was seated in the corner booth, poring over a stack of papers.

"Have a seat, ladies," she said, her eyes flicking up from the paperwork. "I could do with something to distract me from these invoices. I swear, they multiply every time I turn my back."

They slid into the booth. A waitress sauntered over and asked for their order. Donna went with a white wine spritzer. Edy told her that she'd have the same. Donna went with her usual James Bond martini: vodka with a lemon twist, shaken not stirred. The waitress departed, and they made small talk until she returned a minute or two later with their drinks. Donna took one sip, then got down to business.

"Edy, what do you know about illegal diamonds?" she asked. "Specifically, illegal diamonds with a connection to Seth Romero."

Edy shrugged. "Not much. I'm a point of contact for the agency, but I don't investigate. That's your gig, sister. I just keep my eyes and ears open. But just because I haven't heard or seen anything about diamond smuggling doesn't mean it isn't happening. And if it is, you can guess a guy like Romero is involved. I hope you didn't drive all the way into town just for that. Not that I don't love hanging out with you ladies."

"I wish we were just here to ask a few questions," Donna said. "The fact is that I just shot Seth Romero in the face."

Edy's eyes widened. She looked at Taryn, who nodded gravely.

"Should have killed the son of a bitch," Donna continued. "But my shot was wide left by an inch or two, so I only wounded him."

"It would have been better for you if you did kill him," Edy said. "Best you can hope for now is a pair of crutches or a wheelchair. He's not known for letting bygones be bygones. What does your boss have to say about it?"

"That's just the thing," Donna said. "Romero sent a couple of hit men after us. We sent them packing, but not before they cut the phone line at our house. We need to get in touch with Rowdy."

Edy nodded. "How about we go somewhere more private to make that call? You can use my office phone."

They slid out of the booth and headed for a door marked "Employees Only." The bartender, a sullen blonde wearing way too much makeup, gave them the stink-eye as they passed her. Donna shrugged it off. Tending bar in a joint like this was bound to take a toll.

Jimmy John Jackson had been with the Southern Cable Sports Network for the past six seasons. The former starting quarterback for UCLA and the Tampa Bay Buccaneers, he'd seen his career as a player cut short by a series of brain-rattling hits. One more concussion and he'd be pissing himself and forgetting his name. At least that's what his doctor had intoned with all the mirth of an undertaker. Jimmy told that story to anyone who'd listen. Well, maybe that was paraphrasing the doc's actual words, but Jimmy preferred his version to all that medical mumbo-jumbo. Vocabulary aside, the point of the story was that he'd landed a cushy gig with SCSN as a color commentator. All things considered, it was a hell of a lot easier than playing professional football.

"Sorry I'm late, boss," he said, slapping Whitey Andrews on the shoulder as he passed the producer's table. "Got waylaid by a couple hula girls in the hotel lobby. I tried to juke them, but I guess I've lost a step since hanging up my cleats."

Whitey was too busy chatting up Charlotte O'Daniel to respond with anything more than a wave of the hand.

"Come on, Charlotte baby," Whitey pleaded. "I promised I'd get you that audition for *Days of Our Lives*, and I will. I just need a little time is all."

Jimmy shook his head as he headed for his table, where two extra-large human beings were already waiting for him.

Jimmy John Jackson—or Triple J, as his fans called him—was in Hawaii for the NFL's preseason publicity blitz. More specifically, he was in Edy's Bar and Grill to do a little background on two rookie linemen from Seattle. He preferred to go into interviews prepared. You never knew with these guys. Some of them, you had to practically drag the words out of them, while others couldn't shut the fuck up. It only took him a minute to realize these two lunkheads belonged to the former camp. This interview was going to have all the glitz and excitement of a dental procedure.

Even for an eternal optimist like Triple J, this was shaping up to be a long week. Still, it was hard to get too worked up in a place like this. So he settled for explaining his vitamin regimen to the two big men, whose contributions to the conversation were limited to monosyllabic grunts between bites of their double hot fudge sundaes.

"Look here, fellas." Triple J showed them a handful of pills. "Add these to your daily regimen, and you'll have that special bright green urine that will make you the envy of lesser men the world over."

The linemen looked at each other then back at Triple J.

"Think I'll just stick to ice cream," one of the linemen said.

Triple J sighed. He threw his vitamin pills into his mouth and washed them down with a long drink from his bottle of mineral water.

The bartender with too much makeup was named Michelle, and like her boss, she kept her eyes and ears open for any gossip about Hawaii's criminal underworld. Unlike her boss, Michelle didn't report to a law enforcement agency. Instead, she reported to Seth Romero. For the most part, it was just a matter of listening in on Edy's phone calls, then passing along any pertinent information to Romero's organization. It was easy work that paid well. Occasionally, the job required more direct action. Michelle didn't mind that part of the gig either. Sometimes it was fun to get your hands dirty.

When Edy passed the bar with the two blonde feds in tow, Michelle waited until they were out of sight then inserted a device that looked much like a hearing aid into her ear. It was state of the art technology, a listening device remotely connected to a bug in Edy's office as well as one connected directly to the phone line. Michelle could eavesdrop on private phone calls without ever walking out from behind the bar. Hell, she could even mix drinks while listening in on her boss' conversations. Easy-peasy, as Michelle liked to say.

From the sound of things, this was one conversation that she couldn't afford to miss. Edy and her fed friends were talking to another pair of feds on speaker phone, which meant the signal was coming in loud and clear through the earpiece. Even with the ambient dining room noise and the piped-in exotica music, Michelle could understand every word, from both the women in the office and their male counterparts on the other end of the line.

As she listened, she washed and polished the bar's collection of shot glasses and mentally prepared the transcript she'd hand over to Romero's people. It was like envisioning the script of some radio drama. The stars were even kind enough to introduce themselves before the scene started in earnest. The two male agents, who both had the voices and verbal mannerisms of real macho stud types, were named Rowdy and Jade. Seriously. It was enough to make Michelle roll her eyes. Were these clowns federal agents or professional wrestlers? She shook off the thought and forced herself to pay attention to the drama playing out in the restaurant's rear office:

Rowdy: Diamonds stolen. Seth Romero shot. You girls have had a hell of a day.

Jade: You know, we like a couple of Romero's hitters for the murder of those two Molokai cops. Those poor bastards never knew what hit them. They'd stumbled onto something on the Daioo property. My guess is part of Romero's drug operation.

Rowdy: Seth Romero is definitely playing hardball in your backyard.

Donna: Taryn and I are living proof of that.

Rowdy: You're also proof that Seth Romero is directly involved. Listen, I want both of you to stay with Edy tonight. We'll jump on the first plane out of LAX. Donna, first thing tomorrow morning, go take a look at Romero's beach house. Do a little surveillance, but keep your distance. Diamonds or no diamonds, you're bound to be on his hit list now. Edy, I want you to stay at the restaurant. Business as usual, okay? No reason to tip our hand and let Romero know we're onto him. We'll meet up with you as soon as we can. Oh, and by the way, we will bring our trunk of toys. Bang bang, pow pow.

Jade: Oh, Edy? Speaking of toys, I can't wait to see yours.

(laughter)

Rowdy: Bye, girls.

Jade: See you later.

(phone call ends)

Donna: Well, ladies, I guess we have ourselves a game plan.

Michelle removed the listening device from her ear and dropped it into her purse. When the three women emerged from the office, they were giggling like high schoolers on a Friday night. Michelle thought she might puke, but she forced herself to smile at them as they paused in front of the bar. Edy excused herself to get back to work, while the two blondes perched on barstools and ordered a fresh round of drinks. Same cliché bullshit as before: a white wine spritzer for the one named Donna and a James Bond martini for the one named Taryn.

Once they got their drinks, the women turned around on their stools, leaning their backs against the bar. A couple tipsy men in business suits made a half-assed attempt at hitting on them but were rebuffed with a few bitchy words.

"Hey," the one named Donna said, elbowing her friend in the ribs, then gesturing towards a table across the restaurant. "Isn't that Jimmy John Jackson over there?"

The one named Taryn craned her neck. "Where?"

"Over there with those two guys who are built like brick shithouses."

"Oh, my God," Taryn gushed. "I haven't seen him in ages. Not since the Pro Bowl last year."

Michelle followed her line of sight. Donna had been pointing at a table near the front of the restaurant. There were three people seated at a four-top. Ashley had been fawning over them all night, as he did with any famous or semi-famous person who dined at Edy's, so Michelle knew who they were. The two big guys were Billy Morrison and Cordelle Jones-Jordison, a couple of hotshot football players who were in town for some network TV special. They were accompanied by an ex-jock TV personality that Ashley had referred to, repeatedly and with great enthusiasm, as Triple J. His pro athlete days may have been in the rearview mirror, but he still looked to be in good shape. He wasn't built with grotesque proportions like his tablemates, so Michelle figured he must have played a different position. He was also a bit of a pretty boy, with his wavy blonde locks trimmed short on the front and sides but hanging down past his color in the back. His shirt was unbuttoned enough to show the gold chains that dangled between his pumped up pecs. Michelle would have bet her next paycheck that he smelled like deodorant soap and expensive aftershave.

"He was my first fling—well, my only fling—after I was relocated," Taryn said. "I guess that makes him special."

"Well, why don't you go get reacquainted," Donna suggested. "Just remember to keep your wits about you. We're bound to attract some heat after our dance with you-know-who, but it probably won't get too hot until tomorrow."

Taryn placed a hand on her purse. "Don't worry. I'm carrying some heat of my own."

"And don't forget that we have places to be tomorrow morning. Since my man doesn't get here until tomorrow, I'm going back to the hotel and crashing out." Donna reached into her purse and pulled out her wallet. She withdrew a couple bills and handed them to Michelle. "Keep the change, sister."

Michelle thanked her. It was the most generous tip she'd gotten that shift.

Donna slid off her stool and headed for the front door, side-stepping Ashley as she passed the reservation desk. Taryn tossed back the rest of her martini, took a deep breath, and went to meet her boyfriend.

Michelle checked her watch. Her shift was over in fifteen minutes. Then it would be time to check in with Mr. Romero.

"It doesn't look too bad, baby," Rosie said, slipping behind Seth's chair and applying her strong hands to his tense shoulders. "Does it hurt?"

"Never mind that." Seth glanced up at her. "Just keep massaging."

"Really, boss, it's actually going to be a pretty cool scar," Kimo added, leaning back into

the couch and slinging his feet on top of the low coffee table.

"That's not the fucking point!" Seth growled. "That bitch tried to kill me!"

Three stitches on his cheek and a cauterized earlobe. That's what that bitch's bullet had done to his face. His personal doctor had told him the scarring would be minimal, but that wasn't the point. For one thing, *nobody* took a shot at Seth Romero and lived to tell the tale. And for another, he fucking hated needles. Just the thought of them made his asshole pucker.

Now, after he'd swallowed the appropriate painkillers, he was back at his place on Maui, doing his best to relax in his beach bungalow. The twins had refused to let him out of their sight. They were his personal bodyguards, after all, and just hours earlier, there had been an attempt on his life. No way were they going to leave him on his own.

"A little plastic surgery will fix that ear right up," Kimo continued. "That guy who did Rosie's tits really knows his shit. I can get you an appointment if you want."

"Shut up, bro," Rosie hissed as she kneaded Seth's shoulder muscles.

"What?" Kimo shrugged. "The guy was a total pro. You said so yourself."

"Just don't talk about my tits, okay?" Rosie glared at her brother. "It's weird."

"Give it a rest, both of you," Seth said. "I swear, you drive me crazy sometimes."

There was nothing unusual about his best employees annoying him. The truth was, most people annoyed him. Sometimes Seth felt like he was the only person in the world with a functioning brain. Even Rosie, who could reliably anticipate Seth's mood swings, could be a real pain in the ass. But she had other qualities that made the small annoyances worth it.

Over on the little end table at Kimo's right side, the phone started ringing. Seth snapped his fingers and gestured for Kimo to answer it.

Kimo did as instructed, grabbing the cordless receiver and bringing it to his ear. After a moment, he covered the receiver and whispered, "It's Michelle."

Seth sighed. His shoulders refused to relax despite Rosie's forceful ministrations. He doubted talking to that freak Michelle was going to do him much good. Lately, her intel had been nothing but piddling bullshit, and Seth doubted tonight would be any different. Whatever it was she had to say could wait until morning. Maybe then he'd been in a more sociable frame of mind. Then again, maybe not.

"I don't give a fuck if it's a conference call with the queen of England and the pope," he said. "Take a fucking message."

Kimo took his hand off the receiver. "Hey, Michelle, the boss is sort of busy at the moment. He wants me to take a message."

Seth closed his eyes. Those pills the doc had given him weren't doing shit. Maybe a couple bumps of coke would take the edge off. He kept a small stash for emergency purposes. Sure, he had a hard and fast rule for his employees that forbade any use of the illicit substances they trafficked. But there were certain perks to being the boss, the best of which was that rules didn't apply to him. He did whatever the fuck he wanted whenever the fuck he wanted. Anybody had anything to say about that, they could take it up with the sharks.

Kimo ended the call and dumped the receiver back on the charging cradle. "Boss, I think that tranny bartender is finally earning a paycheck. Wait 'til you hear what she had to say."

"Hey, hot stuff," Taryn said, laying a hand on Triple J's shoulder. "Is this seat taken?"

His eyes widened when he turned in his chair. "Taryn? I tried to give you a call when I got into town a few hours ago, but the line was disconnected. You forget to pay your bill or something?"

"Yeah, something like that."

There was one empty chair and the table, and she took it without waiting for an invitation.

Taryn had a thing for jocks. Yeah, it was shallow or superficial or whatever, but ever since high school, she'd gone for the hot, muscular, athletic type. Personality took a backseat to wide shoulders, sculpted abs, and high performance bedroom skills. In fact, she actually preferred it if they were a little on the dumb side. It made them easy to manipulate. Not that any man was very difficult in that regard. No matter how smart they were, they could be led around by the dick. It was practically a universal constant.

"Let me guess," Taryn said, eyeing the two giants across the table. "You're in town for the figure skating convention, right?"

"No, ma'am," one of them replied. "We play football."

"Oh, I just love soccer," she said.

Jimmy stifled a laugh behind his hand. "Boys, I think you're going to have to excuse us. Me and the lady here got some urgent matters to attend to."

He grabbed her hand and led her across the restaurant and out the front door.

"Soccer, really?" he asked as the emerged into the fresh night air. "You know, you shouldn't pick on a couple of nice boys like that."

Taryn laughed. "I'm sorry, but I just couldn't help myself."

"You're a real piece of work, baby."

"I like to think of it as being cute." She shrugged. "I didn't hear any objections that last time we were together."

"That is one hell of an understatement."

Taryn gave his hand a squeeze. "It's good to see you, Jimmy John."

When he suggested they go for a moonlight stroll, she let him think it was his idea. They bought a couple towels from a convenience store and headed for the beach. It was the sort of pleasant night that would stun most people but was commonplace in Hawaii. The sea breeze was just strong enough to stir their hair, and the sound of the surf was a soothing backdrop to their conversation. They kept it light. Taryn didn't get the idea that Jimmy John was the type to get into deep philosophical discussions, and that was fine by her. Although she found him to be charming and even occasionally witty, she wasn't after him for his brain.

When they came across a secluded cove surrounded by trees and he suggested they find a comfortable spot to rest for a while, Taryn let him believe that he was talking her into something. Then, when they found a nice quiet spot and spread out their towels, he started playing hard to get. Taryn thought it was cute the way he acted sort of shy, so she made the first move, going in for a firm, open-mouthed kiss before slipping out of her blouse and skirt. Once her breasts were out in the open, his shyness melted away. He sprang to his feet and was out of his clothes in seconds flat. Evidence of his excitement was on full display. She grabbed hold of it and pulled him back down to her level. He went right to work, kissing her mouth before moving to her neck, her breasts, and then even lower. She closed her eyes and sighed. Finally, he came up for air. She pushed him onto his back and kissed her way from his chest to his pelvis. She licked her lips then returned the favor, licking and sucking until he was ready for the main event. Then she rolled onto her back and spread her legs.

"You know," Taryn said as he settled himself between her thighs. "I'm normally not this easy."

"Neither am I," he whispered, pressing himself against her.

She gasped at the gentle, insistent pressure of his entry. Like she'd told Donna, it had been a while. But Jimmy John knew what he was doing, and he started slow. Taryn relaxed, letting him find his rhythm. Then, at her urging, his thrusts became harder, faster. She bit his shoulder as she shuddered to a climax.

"Not yet, baby," she said when she felt him begin to shake.

Gripping his hips, she rolled him onto his back and climbed atop him. He reached up to run his hand over her breasts as she lowered herself onto him. It didn't take long for her to get back to the edge of explosion. He moaned beneath her, and she knew that he had reached the end of the line. He closed his eyes and groaned. His thigh muscles stiffened then relaxed as the warm explosion filled her. It was enough to put her over the edge one more time.

They lay next to one another, naked and panting as the tide came in, the frothy edges of the water reaching their toes.

Finally, he broke the silence. "Babe, you're pretty damn awesome, you know that?"

"You're not so bad yourself, Jimmy John." Taryn scratched playfully at his chest, pausing to tweak his nipple.

He rolled over onto one elbow and smiled at her. "But I'm not really Jimmy John. I'm actually a British secret agent. You know, tea and crumpets and all that."

Taryn laughed. "Well, secret agent man, how about buying a girl some breakfast? But not tea and crumpets. I'm more of a pancakes and bacon kind of girl."

Chapter Seven

Rowdy hated flying, so he usually knocked back a Valium with a vodka chaser before he boarded a plane. By the time the plane had taxied and been cleared for takeoff, he was headed for dreamland. This flight to Hawaii was no different. By the time the agency's Learjet 29 had begun its ascent, he was nodding off. He didn't wake until the aircraft made its bumpy landing at Molokai Cargo HQ.

"Good morning, sunshine," Jade boomed from his seat across the aisle. He reached over and gave Rowdy a playful punch on the shoulder. "It's a beautiful day in paradise."

Jade, unlike Rowdy, didn't mind flying one bit. He used the time to practice his meditation skills. It was part of his Zen-master/sensei shtick. Normally, Rowdy found the whole eastern-mystic-in-the-body-of-a-SoCal-surfer act amusing, maybe even endearing, but this was not one of those times.

"How in the hell can you be so happy at this hour of the morning?" Rowdy asked, shaking his head to clear the cobwebs. "It *is* morning, right? I can't keep my time zones straight."

"Time is a human construct. The universe doesn't care about such things. Besides, a couple cups of coffee will change that grumpy outlook," Jade replied. "I know a little café that will fix us right up."

They disembarked in front of the company's maintenance hangar and found their vehicle waiting for them. It was the standard issue agency Jeep with all the bells and whistles. Most importantly, it was fully stocked with a small arsenal, including Rowdy's weapon of choice: a four-barrel mini-rocket launcher. Even with Rowdy's notoriously poor marksmanship, he couldn't miss with that bad boy on his shoulder.

Jade climbed into the driver's seat, shaking his head as he caught sight of the rocket launcher. "I can't believe you're still using that thing. The best gun instructors in the world are at your disposal, yet you still have all the accuracy of a drunk Mr. Magoo. It doesn't make sense, man."

"Bad aim runs in the family. I figure God had to give the Abilene men some sort of flaw, just so the rest of you don't get jealous of our perfection." Rowdy shrugged. "Besides, I happen to like that rocket launcher. Raw power and big explosions… shit, what's not to like?"

It was true that none of the Abilene men had ever possessed anything better than marginal firearm skills. Even Rowdy's celebrated cousin—private detective turned government agent turned Hollywood heartthrob, Cody Abilene—would never be mistaken for a sharpshooter. The mini-rocket launcher was a great equalizer in that regard.

"You know," Rowdy said as Jade fired up the Jeep's engine. "I don't really need guns anyway. My hands are lethal weapons."

"Yeah, I've heard that one before. Now buckle up, grasshopper."

The little café Jade had promised turned out to be a food truck selling Spam musubi, but the coffee was fresh and hot. And Rowdy didn't mind a bit of Spam in his diet. Once his belly was full and there was a decent amount of caffeine stoking his body's engine, his outlook improved considerably, just as Jade had predicted.

They climbed back into the Jeep and headed inland. It was a quiet day on the island. There wasn't another car on the road as they passed through the Molokai Wildlife Park. The plan was to check out Donna's house to make sure it was safe then drop in at Edy's and plot their next move. This case was starting to heat up, and Rowdy was ready for some action.

"You know, I can't wait to see Edy," Jade said. "She's so hot. Nothing like my first wife. She used to mow the lawn stark naked."

"What did the neighbors say?" Rowdy asked.

Jade gave him a side-eyed glance. "They said I married her for her money."

"Well…did you?"

"If you'd ever met Rhonda, you wouldn't need to ask that question."

Rowdy threw back his head and laughed. He never got tired of Jade's stories about his numerous ex-wives. There were seven of them in all, each of them more shrewish and unattractive than the last, at least according to Jade. Rowdy suspected that the stories were outright lies or at least exaggerated. No way a guy like Jade would shack up with anything less than a perfect ten. Zen master or not, the man was a regular Don Juan.

"What the hell is this?" Jade pointed at the windshield. "Some nutcase in the middle of the road."

Rowdy finally managed to get his laughter under control.

"That dude must be smoking some heavy doobies," he said, following Jade's line of sight. "Either that or he's a clown on vacation from the circus."

Rowdy's observation wasn't entirely a joke. It *did* look like the man in the road was performing a circus act. He was riding a skateboard, only instead of standing on the board with his feet, he was doing a handstand. And the way he was dressed, anyone would have at least entertained the idea that the man was a clown. He was wearing three-quarter length pants and an oversized silk shirt, both of which sported outrageous flower patterns. It looked like a bouquet of tropical flowers had puked neon all over him.

"What's he got under his arm?" Jade asked, pointing.

"It's one of those inflatable sex dolls," Rowdy said. He leaned his head out of the Jeep to get a better look as they passed the weirdo. Rowdy got a good look at the guy's face. He looked normal enough, although he had a ridiculous horseshoe mustache.

"I guess California doesn't have a monopoly on weirdos," Jade laughed.

Rowdy turned on the radio and spun the dial until he found a station playing an AC/DC tune. He cranked the volume and sang along.

"Man, you need to chill with those aggressive sounds," Jade said, shaking his head. "How about something mellow?"

"You want to listen to something mellow? Okay, fine, we can take turns with the music." Rowdy poked his partner in the shoulder. "But remember my rule: no Steely Dan. Not now, not ever. I hate that fucking band."

Jade sighed. "One of these days, I'm going to convince you to embrace the Dan."

"Don't hold your breath," Rowdy replied.

Harry Kapua had never considered himself to be the introspective type, but ever since that broad nailed him with her ninja throwing star, he'd been questioning his life choices. Like, how had all his decisions led him to this point? He paused to consider this conundrum as he peered through the binoculars, watching Mike do his handstand skateboarding act right past the two agents in the government-issued Jeep.

Fucking Mike, why did he insist on doing shit like that? Harry lowered the binoculars and climbed into the driver's seat of Pontiac, which was hidden from sight behind a boulder just a few yards from the road. *And what the hell was that stupid blow-up sex doll all about anyway? I swear, that dude has lost his grip on reality.*

Harry fired up the car's engine and pulled up alongside the road to meet Mike, who was still doing his stupid skateboard trick in the middle of the road. Harry should have known better than to let Mike take the reins on this thing. Wouldn't it have just been easier to lay a spike strip across the road then machine gun these two pretty boy agents after the Jeep's tires blew? But no, that was too easy. Mike said it lacked style. And as usual, Harry went along with it. Why? Because that was the easiest thing to do, and Harry like things that way.

Maybe I went into the wrong line of work, he thought. *I might have made a good cruise director, teaching sunburned tourists from Iowa how to dance the hula and sing along to Don Ho songs. Maybe find a hot waitress or bartender to shack up with below decks...*

Mike brought the skateboard to a stop alongside the car. He dismounted with a handspring that nearly put him on his ass, but he managed to keep his balance. Although no one was there to applaud—Harry knew that it would only encourage him—Mike took a bow.

"Alright, big boy, give me the shotgun," Mike said, climbing into the passenger seat. "I'm going to teach these assholes a lesson."

Figuring that there was no option other than allowing this stupidity to play out, Harry pulled onto a dirt road and headed for the cutoff point a couple miles ahead. Mike wanted to meet the agents head-on and fire the kill shots from his skateboard. He'd actually asked Harry to capture the event on his camcorder, but that's where Harry drew the line. Letting Mike have his way with his skateboard antics was stupid, but filming a double homicide was fucking bonkers.

Harry gunned the engine, kicking up a whirlwind of dust on

his way to the cutoff. Upon arrival, Mike bailed out and mounted his skateboard. He had his shotgun in one hand and his sex doll in the other.

"Don't you think you better leave that doll in the car?" Harry asked.

"No way." Mike shook his head. "I want Sexy Sally to get a good long look at how I handle a couple of narcs. She gets a front row seat."

Harry sighed. He was beginning to think Mike not be the most stable dude. He'd just given his inflatable sex doll a name. Sexy Sally, for crying out loud.

"Now find a good spot to watch this action, brother," Mike said. "You're about to see something you ain't never seen before, I guarantee it."

"Yeah, sure." Harry tried to summon a smile but couldn't quite do it. He wondered if cruise directors ever regretted their life choices. Like, did those dudes ever sit down and wonder what life was like as a low-level enforcer for a criminal organization? Somehow, Harry doubted it.

Mike kicked off and gained speed quickly as he rode downhill. Harry grabbed his binoculars and prepared himself to watch the stupidity unfold. And sure enough, it didn't take long for Mike to start acting the fool. He started zigzagging as he went downhill, pretending to do the tango with his inflatable girlfriend.

When that chick smashed his nose on her knee, she must have scrambled his brains, Harry thought. *This dude is turning into an actual moron, like in the true sense of the word.*

The Jeep was also gathering speed as it reached the valley between two hills. They had to swerve to avoid turning Mike into a greasy spot on the road. It slowed their approach just enough for Mike to open up with his shotgun. The first blast missed the target altogether, blowing a hole in the Jeep's hood. The second hit the driver, knocking him back in his seat. Harry couldn't tell if it was a kill shot, but he wouldn't have bet on it. Knowing their luck, Mike probably just grazed the guy.

So much for style points, dumbass, Harry thought.

Mike sailed past the Jeep, then brought the skateboard to a skidding halt. Without loosening his hold on the sex doll—Sexy Sally herself—he broke open the double barrel shotgun and dumped the spent shells. He grabbed a couple fresh ones from his shirt's breast pocket and dropped them into the barrels. But all that fucking around on the skateboard had given the other agent the opportunity to grab a weapon from the backseat and draw a bead on Mike.

Harry's eyes bulged behind the binoculars' eyepieces. The dude had a goddam four-barrel bazooka! The wounded driver had recovered enough to bring the Jeep around and start driving straight at Mike. Meanwhile, his partner took aim with his shoulder canon.

What the hell, brah? Harry wondered aloud. *That Rambo shit can't be real.*

But it was real, all right. The Jeep hit Mike head-on before he could fire the shotgun. The impact sent him airborne. Harry figured he must have been about fifteen feet in the air. Like, the due was *flying*. As Mike reached peak altitude, the agent with the bazooka let one of the rockets fly. It was a bullseye shot that reduced Mike to bloody chunks and pink mist. Amazingly, Sally survived the explosion. A sudden gust of wind carried her up into the sky like a kite. But the agent with the bazooka didn't take mercy on Mike's rubber girlfriend. A second rocket blast erupted from one of the bazooka's four barrels, and poor Alice was consumed in a fiery explosion. Like, she was fucking vaporized.

Harry lowered the binoculars and slumped down behind the Pontiac's steering wheel. No paycheck was worth this bullshit.

Most large constrictors—a python, for example—don't range much further than a mile on any given day. But the mutant monster that had escaped from the Brazilian weapons laboratory was no ordinary constrictor. Its immense size belied the speed with which it could cover open ground. And in the early morning hours, it had uncoiled in its warm hiding place in the septic system below Donna Hamilton's house and emerged into the warmth of the Molokai sunrise, ready to seek out new and interesting prey.

Its voracious appetite had been reawakened, and as it made its way toward Kapukahehu beach, it consumed two rodents and three birds. As far snacks went, these morsels were just fine. But they were hardly enough to satisfy the snake's hunger. It forged ahead, over patches of rocky terrain and through moist stretches of dense vegetation, spurred on by some strange sixth sense that told it prey lay just a few miles ahead. And this was the best prey of all: human prey.

Joey Gilbert wanted to make the most of the time he and Jamie had left at their secluded campsite just off Kapukahehu beach. The prior day had been simply magical. Once the two pilots had departed, he and Jamie had stripped off their clothes and gone for a swim. For a couple of kids from Shelbyville, Indiana, a nude dip in the Pacific was an unparalleled thrill. They'd emerged from the water, still dripping wet as they made love atop a blanket spread on the sun-warmed sand. At sunset, they'd built a campfire and cooked hot dogs over the flames. After dinner, they'd made love under the stars, their moans of pleasure mingling with the chorus of tree frogs. Upon waking at daybreak, they'd gone at it again, testing the limits of their flexibility with unfamiliar positions. After breakfast, Jamie had begun to look at Joey with that special twinkle in her eye, but he'd suggested they take a break from the amorous workouts.

Frankly, he was a bit sore. Doing the deed on the beach was a great idea on paper—and yeah, it had been pretty damn thrilling—but sand had a way of insinuating itself into all the bodily crevices.

"Hey, babe, how about we try something else?" he suggested.

"Like what?" Jamie stretched her arms over her head languidly.

Joey had to remind himself that his new bride was the same girl who taught kindergarten and sang in the church choir back home. It was an amazing transformation, like something out of a nature program on TV. The metamorphosis of the All-American Sweetheart into an insatiable sex kitten.

"Maybe we could take some pictures," Joey said.

They'd brought their Polaroid camera with them, and Joey thought it would be fun to stage a bikini photo shoot on the beach. The camera had been a gift from his aunt Lurlene, and Joey thought it could capture his wife's radiant beauty. At the very least, it would give him something to look at when he was away on a business trip and needed to get rid of some work-related stress. So Jamie had donned the string bikini she'd purchased at a gift shop near Waikiki, teased her hair as best she could with the minimal supply of beauty products in her backpack, and struck her best swimsuit model poses.

"That's great, baby," Joey said, snapping a shot. He pulled the photo from the camera and dropped it atop the growing pile between his feet. "Now really turn it on. Show me how sexy you are!"

Jamie arched her back and ran her hands over her breasts.

Joey peered through the viewfinder and captured the moment. Sore or not, he felt the first twitches and tingles of arousal in his shorts. It still seemed like a dream. How did a guy like him manage to land a woman like Jamie? She was the perfect woman: not just sexy, but also caring, kind, and genuinely sweet. She didn't even mind watching football on autumn Saturdays.

"How's this for sexy?" Jamie asked, reaching behind her shoulders to untie her bikini top.

Those twitches and tingles in his shorts were growing more insistent as Joey took another snapshot.

"Sexy enough for you?" Jamie asked as she removed the bottom half of her bathing suit.

"Oh, yeah…"

"You're pretty good at doing two things at once," she purred. "Think you can take photos and make love at the same time?"

Joey had always figured the stories he read in *Penthouse* were bullshit, but now that he was experiencing one of them in real life, he began to wonder what other thrills might be possible. He added another photo to the pile, then watched open-mouthed and wide-eyed as Jamie strode forward and dropped to her knees in front of him. She untied the drawstring on his shorts and tugged them down.

"I know you're sore, baby," she said. "But don't worry, I'll be gentle."

Joey angled the camera downwards and captured the moment for posterity. Had he known it would be the last photo he'd ever take, he would have said that there sure as hell were worse ways to go. But since he didn't hear the faint rustle of the snake emerging from the tree line, he never knew that he had only seconds to live.

He looked down, watching his bride go to work on him. As she brought him to full attention, he closed his eyes and sighed, wondering if married life would always be so pleasant. This reverie came to an abrupt end as the snake sunk its fangs into the back of his leg, pumping a full ounce of concentrated neurotoxin into his calf muscle. It only took a few seconds for the convulsions to drop him to the sand. By then, he was deaf to the sound of his wife's screams. And really, that was for the best. In the midst of nature's cruelty, there were small moments of mercy.

The shotgun blast had done a number on the Jeep's engine, but it limped along enough to get to the nearest hospital. When Rowdy twisted the key in the ignition and felt the vehicle shudder violently, he knew it wasn't leaving the parking lot unless it was being pulled behind a tow truck.

"Well, guess that about does it for our badass government vehicle," Rowdy said, slapping the dashboard. He turned to Jade, who was bleeding all over the passenger seat. "All right, buddy, how you feeling?"

Jade smiled. "All things being equal, I'd rather be on the beach with a Mai Tai in my hand, but I guess I'll survive."

"That's the spirit." Rowdy climbed out of the Jeep, trotted around to the passenger side, and helped Jade disembark.

The Emergency Room lobby was nearly empty. Must have been a slow day for injuries on the island. The charge nurse slapped an ID wristband on Jade and escorted him through a set of doors. A grandmotherly type with her grey hair pulled into a tight bun atop her head, she spoke in soft tones, telling Jade he'd soon be right as rain.

Rowdy left the ER and went back to the Jeep, which was still venting thin trails of noxious smoke. The engine may have been royally fucked, but the car phone was still in working order. Rowdy used it to call Edy's Bar and Grill. The proprietor of the establishment was one of the agency's best civilian contacts in Hawaii, after all. And, as Jade was so fond of pointing out, she was awful easy on the eyes.

"Edy's Bar and Grill." The voice that answered the phone had a soft Southern lilt to it. Rowdy wondered if that accent belonged to some southern belle transplanted to the islands. He imagined someone blonde, buxom, and sweet as the iced tea of his childhood. But he tamped down his imagination and reminded himself that there was serious business to attend to.

"Hey, I need to speak to Edy," he said. "I know she's probably busy, but this is an urgent matter. Tell her it's Rowdy."

"You got it, sweetheart," the voice on the other end of the line answered.

Rowdy endured a brief period of Muzak that played while his call was on hold. Finally, Edy answered.

"Rowdy," she said. "Where are you? I was starting to get worried. I thought you'd be here by now."

"It's a good news/bad news situation," he explained. "We're at the hospital. Now, before you get yourself all worked up, we're okay. That's the good news. Bad news is that the Jeep the agency provided for us is as dead as Elvis."

"Oh my God." Despite his warning, she sounded all worked up. "What happened?"

"Let's just say the welcoming committee lacked that old Aloha spirit."

"Stay put," Edy said. "I'll come pick you up and you can tell me all about it."

"Sure thing." Rowdy ended the call and made his way back to the waiting room.

He killed some time leafing through last month's issue of *Cosmopolitan*. Jade emerged from the back of the emergency room before Rowdy could make it through the quiz that promised to match his lovemaking style to his astrological sign. He supposed it would just have to remain one of the mysteries of the universe.

He tossed the magazine onto the chair next to him and stood up. "Okay, my man, what's the word?"

"Well, the doc said that I'm going to be sore for a while," Jade answered, tugging his shirt aside to display his bandaged chest. "However, there was this great looking nurse in there and she was extremely helpful. She took my mind off the whole ordeal."

"Oh yeah?" Rowdy raised an eyebrow. "And how exactly did she manage that?"

Jade smiled. "She kept me in stitches the whole time."

"Man, that's a new low, even for you," Rowdy groaned. "I guess Johnny Carson's job is secure for the moment. Come on, let's get out of here. Edy's on her way to give us a lift into town."

Once again, Michelle found herself listening in on one of Edy's phone calls and mentally preparing a transcript. She recognized the caller's voice right away. It was Rowdy, one of the agents from last night's phone call. Her mind's eye conjured up a mental image to go with the voice. He was probably tall, dark, and handsome, a real square-jawed All-American hero type with big muscles and an even bigger ego. Michelle wondered if there was any other part that waas big, just to complete the package. She sighed inwardly. It didn't matter what Rowdy looked like. He'd never waste time with someone like her. And not just because she was a criminal and he was a Johnny Law. Michelle just wasn't like other girls.

She shook herself out of her daydream and started taking mental notes. It sounded like Harry and Mike hadn't been able to knock off these two agents after all. Michelle would hate to be the one to break the news to Mr. Romero. However, now she knew exactly where those two agents were.

Edy came out of her office just long enough to let Michelle know she had some errands to run and would probably be gone for most of the day.

"Isn't that a coincidence?" Michelle said. "I feel a migraine coming on. Is it okay if I get Carla to cover my shift so I can go home and sleep it off?"

Edy nodded. "Yeah, that's fine. Get to feeling better, sister."

Michelle waited until Edy was out of there before grabbing the phone and placing two calls. The first was to Carla, who acted like she was being asked to do eight hours of harsh manual labor in the blazing hot sun rather than cover a single shift behind the bar. When Michelle sweetened the deal by offering to introduce her to some of the football players who were in town, Carla's mood improved. The second call was to Rosie, who answered on the first ring.

"Hey, Rosie," Michelle said. "I need you and Kimo to come pick me up as soon as possible. Since Harry and Mike struck out, maybe we can…"

"Change of plan," Rosie interrupted. "Seth wants us to grab your boss instead. We'll be there to pick you up in ten minutes."

Michelle wondered why they would even bother with Edy when they knew where the two feds were. But she knew better than to argue with Seth Romero's plans, even if they appeared nonsensical. The man didn't get to the top of the food chain by following any conventional wisdom. In fact, Michelle didn't even know if he followed any wisdom at all. It was something closer to animal instinct. He acted on impulse. For most people, that would spell disaster, but the god of violent criminals had always favored Seth Romero, and those who questioned this state of affairs didn't live long.

Michelle hung up the phone and headed for the staff lounge. It meant leaving the bar unattended until Carla arrived, but the lunch rush was still at least an hour away.

She grabbed her backpack from her locker and headed for the bathroom. She had just enough time to get changed before Rosie and Kimo arrived.

When she stepped into the women's room, she was met by Sue, the waitress currently pulling down the most tips at the restaurant. Sue was stark naked. As usual, she'd come straight from the beach to work and was using the employee restroom as her personal changing area. Her work clothes were piled on the counter, and she was rinsing the sand out of her bathing suit in the sink.

"Oh, hey, Michelle," she said. "What's up?"

"Got a migraine coming on, so I'm scooting out of here," Michelle answered.

"Yeah, you don't mind me saying so, you don't look so good." Sue lifted one breast and wiped beneath it with a paper towel. She repeated the process with the other one. "You need to get more exercise. Look at me. It takes at least thirty minutes of workout every day to keep these tits looking good. Plus, it helps with your psychology shit too. A healthy body and a healthy mind, that's the right balance."

Michelle gave her a withering look. "I see you're halfway there."

Sue smiled, oblivious as ever. "Remember what I said. Good tits are a hell of an asset."

Michelle thanked her and retreated to a stall while Sue finished up. Once the bimbo waitress had completed her costume change and left, Michelle locked the bathroom door and unzipped her backpack.

First, she shed the blond wig. Next, she removed the fake eyelashes and scrubbed the makeup from her face. Off came the skirt and blouse, along with the bra stuffed with its jiggly fake breasts. Then, sighing with relief, she tugged down the panties and freed her penis from its tucked position. Things could occasionally get uncomfortable down below. That was the price of beauty, she supposed.

"Well, now," she said, spreading her legs so her pride and joy could breathe for a few seconds while she admired herself in the mirror. "Ain't that something?"

She dressed in a pair of blue jeans and a golf shirt, completing the transition from

Michelle to Michael, from she to he. All things considered, Michael was a handsome, if somewhat average, guy. He just happened to also be one hell of a sexy lady. There were plenty of on-again/off-again lovers, both male and female, who could attest to his ability to switch between roles without missing a beat.

He poked his head out of the bathroom to make sure the coast was clear, then made a beeline for the back door of the restaurant, where a black van was idling. Kimo poked his head out of the passenger side window.

"Hey, man," he said, "let's get moving. We ain't got all day."

Michael climbed into the backseat and said, "She's headed for the hospital. Let's grab her before she can hook up with those feds. I know a back road that will help us get ahead and cut her off."

Rosie hit the gas. Following Michael's directions, she whipped the van onto a dusty stretch of sun-bleached asphalt that qualified as a road in only the loosest sense of the word. It was barely wide enough to accommodate the van, but Rosie managed to keep the vehicle out of the ditches that ran along both sides. She floored the accelerator, going as fast as she dared on such a narrow, bumpy track.

"There should be a road…" Michael pointed. "Yeah, up here on the left."

Rosie took the turn so fast that two of the van's tires lifted off the blacktop for one hair-raising moment. Michael gripped the armrests, wishing that he'd remembered to buckle up. Then the van slammed back down on all four tires, testing the limits of the vehicle's already worn-out suspension.

"Now what?" Rosie asked as she wheeled the van onto the highway.

Michael leaned forward to look out the windshield. Edy's car was a half-mile away, heading straight for them.

"See that pink Cadillac? That's our target," he said.

"Better buckle up," Rosie said. "This could get rough."

Michael and Kimo did as she suggested, bracing themselves for the impact that was only seconds away.

The van's reinforced front bumper clipped the Caddy's front quarter panel. It wasn't much more than a love tap, but at those speeds, even a love tap gets big results. The Caddy skidded off the road, kicking up plenty of grit and gravel as it crossed the shoulder. It flew down the steep embankment, coming to an abrupt halt in a patch of loose, sandy soil. Rosie hit the brakes, laying down twin streaks of rubber as the van jolted to a stop. Michael and Kimo ripped off their seatbelts and bailed out. They hit the ground running.

The target was still belted in behind the steering wheel. She was dazed and shaken up, but otherwise unharmed. Michael had to remind himself that this wasn't some stranger they'd run off the road. The target was Edy St. James, who enjoyed cold bottles of Corona with an extra wedge of lime and snorted softly when she laughed at her own jokes. Did he feel a slight twinge of regret? Maybe. Edy was a good boss and seemed to be a kind person. But most of that regret belonged to Michelle. After all, it was Michelle, not Michael, who worked for Edy. That was the good thing about being two people in one body. Compartmentalizing life's more difficult experiences was easier for him than it was for other people. And while Michelle may have developed a soft spot for Edy, Michael was much less sympathetic. The way he saw it, Edy was their target, and that was all there was to it.

Kimo leaned into the car, reached across Edy, and unbuckled her seatbelt. They pulled her out of the car and led her to the van. She was still too dazed by the crash to put up more than token resistance. Still, one can never be too safe in these situations, so Michael handcuffed her all the same.

"Keep calm and do as we say, and you'll be fine," he told her. "Kick up a fuss and you'll get hurt."

Edy glared at him. "Who the hell are you?"

Michael just laughed as he shoved her into the van.

Chapter Eight

The binoculars were intended for bird watching, but Taryn figured they would work for surveillance just fine. Donna had chosen a camcorder with an extra zoom feature. While she wasn't certain any footage she captured would be admissible in court, she was a firm believer in covering all the angles. Get all the evidence you can and let the lawyers and judges sort it out, that was her philosophy.

"How long are we supposed to do this?" Taryn asked. "I mean, Rowdy didn't really give us a timeframe, did he?"

Donna shrugged. "Don't know."

"Because we've been here for a while already."

Donna gave an encore performance of her shrug. This time she limited her response to a noncommittal grunt. The morning had made one thing abundantly clear: Taryn wasn't quite ready for stakeouts. If she ever made it through Donna's ad-hoc field agent training and decided to pursue a job in law enforcement, Taryn was going to need to develop some patience.

The Daioo estate was situated a half-mile inland from the beach. The main house was a sprawling ranch style affair with a manicured front lawn ringed by palm trees and trellises draped in bright green vines. One side of the house was dominated by a sunroom with floor-to-ceiling windows, while the opposite side was a massive, five-car garage. The entire property was surrounded by a low retaining wall made of river stones. There was a wooded patch behind the house, beyond which was the Daioo family's marijuana operation. They were allowed to operate on a limited basis because Herman, the patriarch of the family, was cooperative with the agency's investigation into bigger fish: the cocaine and dope wholesalers who'd been setting up shop on Molokai. Herman was also a big player in state politics, greasing all the right palms to ensure his free pass for weed cultivation remained intact.

Donna knew there was no way Herman or even his half-wit yuppie sons were involved with someone like Seth Romero. She figured that pieces of Herman and the boys would start washing up on shore any day now. And that was a shame. All in all, she liked Herman. He was an old hippie who was perpetually stoned and smiling. It was hard not to find him endearing. If he'd met his end at Romero's hands, it was just one more reason to take Romero down.

Taryn swept the binoculars from the beach to the house on the Daioo estate and then back again. "At least this guy is pretty good with that Frisbee. I don't know if they have a professional league, but he could probably try out for one."

They guy in question was indeed good with the Frisbee that he was tossing back and forth with a female companion. Behind the back catches, under the leg tosses, and single finger hooks, this guy could do it all. But he was no beach bum. He was armed with a submachine gun and had a walkie-talkie clipped to his belt. His sunglasses—a pair of mirrored shades right out of a bad cop movie—were appropriate for the beach, but the rest of his outfit wasn't. Donna had been on Molokai for three years now, and she could attest to the fact that people didn't visit the beach in expensive loafers, khaki trousers, and long sleeved dress shirts.

Taryn decided it was time to state the obvious. "That guy

has a machine gun and a walkie talkie. He could probably call in an army."

"I recognize the girl," Donna said. "She's a local. Works at the Hang Loose Pancake Hut. No way she's involved in anything illegal. Must have met this guy while waiting his table and he invited her out for a day on the beach. Guess even gun thugs get some time off for rest and recreation."

"But what about him carrying that gun? Isn't she scared?"

"Her name's Sandra," Donna explained. "The kitchen guys call her Short Bus Sandra. She's not brain damaged or anything like that, but she's sure as hell not the sharpest tool in the shed. Probably thinks he's some rich tourist with a thing for personal security. Who knows?"

Before Donna could elaborate any further, the steady thrum of a helicopter's rotors cut through the white noise of the surf. The *thump-thump-thump* grew louder and louder as the chopper came into view.

"Looks like we finally got some activity," Taryn said. "That thing is landing right in the front yard."

Donna hit the zoom on her camera, pulling in as tight as she could on the scene unfolding in front of the house. The chopper's door swung open, and a trio of armed thugs jumped out. They dragged a fourth person out, a woman whose hands were bound in front of her. She kicked and struggled as two of the thugs dragged her across the yard. The pilot cut the engine, and the rotors gradually slowed and then stopped altogether.

"Shit," Taryn said as she trained her binoculars on the captive woman's face. "They've got Edy. Come on, let's see if we can creep up and get a closer look."

Crouched low, the two women advanced, keeping themselves hidden behind the sand dunes and the scattered vegetation.

They stopped just short of the house, hiding behind a low retaining wall that ringed the property. The back door of the house swung open, and out walked Seth Romero himself, his face bandaged where Donna's bullet had carved a bloody trench through his cheek. He was followed by an armed guard.

Well, that's just great, Donna thought. *We're outnumbered and outgunned.*

She knew that a daring, spur-of-the-moment rescue might work in the movies, but out in the real world, it would probably just spell disaster. Better to hunker down and listen, assesses the situation.

Romero strutted across the front yard, rubbing his hands together. He was dressed in a pair of white slacks and a vividly patterned silk shirt. When he spoke, his voice was every bit as loud as the colors on his shirt. Donna could hear every word he said.

"At last, my orders are finally obeyed!" Romero clapped his hands. He slapped one of the thugs on the back. "Thank you, my man."

The thug nodded. Donna thought his face looked familiar, but she couldn't quite place it. And it wasn't just his face that was familiar. The ruby and sapphire pinkie ring on his left hand was distinctive enough to catch Donna's eye. She was sure she'd seen it somewhere before. But where and when? The answers were just out of reach, tickling her brain like a cross-word puzzle clue that should have been easy but nevertheless remained elusive.

"You see that guy on the left?" Donna whispered, pointing at the strangely familiar man.

"Nope," Taryn replied, shaking her head. "He some famous criminal or something?"

Donna shrugged. "I don't know. He just looks really familiar for some reason. Something about his face. And check out that ring. That ring a bell with you?"

"It's the sort of tacky shit my ex-husband used to buy me when he was feeling guilty about cheating on me," Taryn said. "Other than that, I don't know."

Meanwhile, Romero had turned his attention to Edy. He

loomed over her, fists planted on his hips. Donna cocked her head to one side as she listened.

"So, I hear you've been poking your nose into my business," Romero barked. "That's a big mistake. People who do that sort of thing come to bad ends. Maybe if you tell me where I can find the rest of my diamonds, that won't have to happen to you."

Edy shook her head furiously. "I don't know what you're talking about."

"Don't bother denying it," he snapped. "But don't worry, I have plans for you."

The group of armed guards dragged Edy into the house. Romero lingered outside for a moment, gazing out at the ocean while he gently probed his wounded cheek. Donna wished her bullet had done more damage. A few inches difference, and this whole mess would already be over and done with.

Finally, Romero finished daydreaming about whatever it was the murderous drug lords daydreamed about and walked into the house he'd stolen from Herman Daioo.

Donna looked at Taryn and said, "We better get Rowdy and Jade out here quick."

Once they were sure they unobserved, they beat a hasty retreat down the beach. When they came to the trailhead leading up to a scenic overlook, they turned off the beach and onto the packed dirt path through the woods. They hiked the path like a couple of tourists, only they didn't pause for any snapshots of the local flora and fauna. It was only a mile and change to the small parking lot where they'd left the Jeep. They climbed into the vehicle and pointed it in the direction of town.

Once Donna had the Jeep on a straight stretch of road, she turned to Taryn and said, "You know a place we can find a phone?"

Taryn nodded. "Take a left at the four way stop. There's a little cinderblock building about a half mile down the road. I think they have a phone we can use."

Donna wasn't sure what sort of place she was expecting, but it certainly wasn't Kimosuki's Sumo Academy. She wheeled the Jeep into the parking lot and got a space near the front door.

"Really, Taryn? A sumo wrestling school?" she asked.

"Well, sometimes I like to watch a few matches while you're out on assignment," Taryn said. "I mean, there's only so many movies a girl can watch before she gets bored."

A stone-faced man roughly the size of a small mountain greeted them at the front desk. The chair he was sitting on must have been made of high-tensile steel and concrete to support him. Donna looked over his shoulder into the main room of the building, where a couple of similarly oversized men in what appeared to be cloth diapers were shoving one another around on a gym mat.

"Let me handle this," Taryn said. "Like my man James Bond, I'm fluent in many languages. I can communicate with people from all cultures."

Donna knew this was nowhere near the truth, but she kept that herself and watched Taryn sidle up to the desk.

"*Excuse-ay moi, senor,*" Taryn spoke each syllable slowly and loudly. She mimed dialing, then talking on a telephone, as she delivered an attempt at some sort of foreign language. Donna winced as Taryn cleared her throat and said, "Me and *mon amigo yo quiero uno telefono el por favor. Necessario to callioso mis amigos por fromage un compleanno…*"

The wrestler's impassive expression didn't twitch as he listened to this monologue. Taryn cleared her throat and plowed on. "*Yo quiero uno queso fratello avec el pallacanestro…*"

Donna glanced around the room and found a doorway with a "Restrooms" sign above it. She disengaged herself from Taryn's attempt at foreign relations and headed through the doorway. Sure enough, there was a pay phone at the end of the hallway, just past the restrooms. She dug a dime out of her purse and dropped it in the slot. She dialed the number for Edy's Bar and Grill.

"Yo, this is Molokai's hippest spot, Edy's Bar and Grill, where the cocktails are always cold and the action is always hot, hot, hot. Feel like making a reservation?"

Donna rolled her eyes at the sound of Ashley's voice, then said, "Ashley, it's Donna. Is Rowdy or Jade there?"

"Sorry, my lady," Ashley answered. "But your boyfriends haven't graced us with their presence today. And the boss ain't here neither, so I'm the captain of this ship for now."

"Damn. Well, if any of them happen to show up, tell them to head out to my place. It's important, so don't forget."

"Hey, who do you think you're talking to here? I'll have them call you as soon as I see their smiling faces," Ashley said.

"They can't call," Donna explained. "Our phone is still out of order. Just tell them to get out there ASAP."

"No problem, hot stuff. Anything else I can help you with?"

Donna thought for a moment, then asked, "That bartender Michelle isn't there, is she?"

"No, that weird chick took off earlier. Must have been that time of the month, you know? Hormones all out of whack or something like that. Why you asking about her?"

Finally, Donna knew why Romero's hired gun had looked so familiar.

"No reason in particular," she said. "Thanks, Ashley."

She went down the hallway and grabbed Taryn, escorting her out of the building and sparing the behemoth behind the desk any more of Taryn's Spanish or French or whatever the hell language she was butchering.

"Hey, I think I was starting to get through to him," Taryn protested as she climbed into the Jeep.

Donna rolled her eyes. "Listen, I finally figured out why that guy with Romero looked so familiar. He's Michelle, the bartender from Edy's. I knew I recognized that pinkie ring. Romero must have known Edy was spying on him and put Michelle...or whatever his name is...there to keep tabs on her. That's why all her tips lately haven't panned out."

Taryn's brow wrinkled. "So the girl is a guy. And the guy is a plant."

"You're catching on," Donna said. "Now buckle up so we can get out of here. We may be doing super dangerous secret agent stuff, but we still have a couple of honeymooners from Indiana that are waiting for us to pick them up."

"Damn, I almost forgot about Joey and Jamie." Taryn slapped her forehead. "Those two lovebirds are probably dying to get back to civilization by now."

Rowdy checked his watch for second time in the last couple minutes. He'd done so much pacing around the parking lot in the last hour that he was surprised he hadn't worn a rut in the asphalt. Jade, on the other hand, appeared as cool, calm, and collected as ever. He sat atop the hood of the broken down Jeep and practiced his meditation.

Rowdy paused in front of the Jeep and watched his partner for a moment. He couldn't decide if he was impressed or annoyed by Jade's apparent tranquility. Maybe it was a mixture of both. At any rate, it was time to put a stop to the zen master stuff and get back to work. He put his foot on the front bumper and rocked the Jeep until Jade opened his eyes and untangled his legs from the lotus position.

"Yes, grasshopper?" Jade yawned.

"It's been an hour," Rowdy said. "Even if there was a traffic jam, Edy still should have been here by now. I'm starting to get worried. Are you worried?"

"What do you suggest?"

Rowdy wondered how much of Jade's tranquil demeanor was an effect of his meditation and how much was down to the painkillers in his system.

"I suggest we grab our gear and try to hitch a ride into

town," Rowdy said. "It's a short walk back to the highway, and there's bound to be some traffic at this time of day."

Jade nodded. "That sounds like a wise course of action."

They grabbed their weapons case and luggage from the back of the Jeep. Rowdy had to carry most of it to allow Jade to rest his injured shoulder. He was suddenly thankful for all the extra hours he'd put in at the gym this year. He knew all that hard work would pay off with the ladies, but he'd never counted on harsh manual labor. The half-mile to the highway felt like a death march with all that extra weight on his back. But there was a pair of trees at the intersection, and the two agents stood in the shade while they waited for someone to pick them up.

They didn't have to wait long. Rowdy had barely had time to stretch his aching back when an old-fashioned Airstream RV pulled onto the shoulder of the road just ahead of them. The driver's side window lowered and a man poked his head out. He was an older gentleman with a head full of slicked-back grey hair. He wore a pair of Elvis-style gold sunglasses and a single gold earring in his left ear. He smiled broadly, revealing a pair of gold incisors that perfectly matched his accessories.

"You boys need a lift?" he called.

The Airstream backfired, farting out a cloud of black smoke.

"Well," Jade said, shrugging as he glanced at Rowdy. "Beggars can't be choosers, right?"

"Yeah, but it's just our luck to have to ride with some weirdo." Rowdy gathered their luggage. "Luckily, it's just a short ride to Edy's."

They popped the hatch on the luggage compartment and crammed their stuff inside. There wasn't much space available. The compartment was packed with mismatched suitcases and bags. The guy with the Elvis shades certainly didn't travel light.

"Come on, fellas," the man with the sunglasses called. "We ain't got all day."

Rowdy and Jade strolled up to the driver's side window.

"Thanks for stopping," Rowdy said.

"Shit, it ain't nothing." The man's smile widened. "Name's Max. Max Meehan."

Rowdy shook his hand and made introductions for himself and Jade.

"Well, climb on in," Max said. "Might be a little tight in the back, but I don't reckon you boys will mind getting close to my passengers."

"Passengers?" Rowdy opened the rear door. His eyes widened at the sight of Max's passengers. "Wow, I mean…yeah, we don't mind the tight fit."

Jade peered over his shoulder. "It will be rough, but I think we can manage somehow."

The rear portion of the RV was filled with a dozen women, each of them clad in a few scraps of fabric that could generously be described as a bathing suit. Half of them hadn't even bothered with the top portions of their bikinis. Rowdy figured that all the fabric combined might be enough for a decent shirt for a small child. Each of the women wore a headband adorned with fake cat ears and sported Lone Ranger-style masks in various feline fur patterns.

"Say hello to Max's Foxy Felines," Max said. "We're in town to shoot our annual bathing beauty swimsuit calendar and maybe have a little fun besides. You boys aren't too busy, we got a party going on at the Sheraton tonight. Just clean yourselves up a bit beforehand. You don't mind me saying, you look like you got rolled by a gang of punks."

The women giggled and meowed.

Rowdy and Jade exchanged a look.

"As fun as that sounds, we're all tied up with work at the moment," Rowdy said. Declining such an invitation was a source of near-physical pain. He figured the regret would fade in time, but probably not for years.

"Hate to hear it," Max said. "But climb on in and make yourselves comfortable."

Rowdy didn't think that getting comfortable would be a problem.

Donna didn't know what to expect from the honeymooning Gilberts. Some people really took to beach camping and had to practically be dragged back to civilization. Others couldn't deal with even one night in the elements and couldn't wait to return to soft beds, electricity, and running water. Neither reaction would have surprised her. But her reaction to what she and Taryn found at the campsite went far beyond surprise.

"Donna..." Taryn gasped, gazing down at the bloody sand. "What do you think happened?"

"I don't know..." Donna glanced around, trying assess the extent of the carnage.

"They're all torn up," Taryn muttered. "I mean, my God, it's terrible."

Both Joey and Jamie were lying lifeless amid the ruins of their campsite. Their bodies looked like they'd been pulverized by some sort of industrial machinery. Jagged ends of broken bones protruded from their abdomens. Their limbs were bent and twisted at unnatural angles. Joey's head had been twisted around backwards, so that his chin rested between his shoulder blades. His tongue protruded between bloody lips. The tip of it appeared to have been bitten off.

Jamie hadn't fared much better against whatever crazed person or animal had attacked them. Her chest had been ripped open. Flies swarmed over her exposed organs. Her right arm was gone below the elbow. Donna found it a few yards away, lying in the sand. Crabs scuttled over it, picking at the blood-crusted flesh.

"You don't think this was Romero's work, do you?" Taryn asked.

"I don't think so," Donna replied. "He's a murderous

psycho, that's for sure. But he's also all about his business. There's no angle here for him. The Gilberts were just random civilians. They weren't informants or witnesses. Unless they saw something they shouldn't have, but that's doubtful out here. We're a few miles from the Daioo estate."

"Hey, I think I found something that might help us figure this out," Taryn said.

Donna turned away from the appalling spectacle of the crabs devouring human flesh and saw Taryn approaching with something in her hand.

"It's a camera," Taryn said, handing the Polaroid to Donna. "It was over there on the ground by their tent. There was a pile of photos scattered around. Looks like they were having some fun taking naughty pictures when…well, when whatever happened. Looks like there's one jammed in there."

Donna worked her fingers into the narrow aperture and pinched the white portion of the instant photo. She tugged gently, careful not to tear it as she worked it loose from the camera.

"Oh, man," Taryn said as Donna finally freed the photo. "It looks like it's starting to develop."

Donna gave the photo a shake and watched as colors blossomed on the glossy surface of the photo. Gradually, the image began to take shape.

"Is that what I think it is?" Taryn asked.

Donna nodded. "No mistaking something that ugly."

The photo was blurry portrait of a monstrous snake. The same snake that had escaped from a crate in their garage. The same snake that Glen Dickson had warned them was so dangerous. Its hideous head filled most of the frame. Its jaws were freakishly distended to reveal a glistening set of fangs.

"You don't think that thing's still hanging around here, do you?" Taryn's face was pale, her eyes wide with fear.

Donna shook her head. "I don't know, but I don't intend to

find out. Let's beat it before it decides to come back. We can call this in to the local cops and let them handle it."

Chapter Nine

Ashley McBride didn't just think he was the cock of the walk; he knew it for a fact. All the action he got was a testament to his status as the Don Juan of Molokai. In fact, he liked that little nickname so much he was considering having business cards made. Okay, fair enough, he'd made up that nickname himself, but sooner or later it was bound to catch on. At any given moment, there were probably dozens of ladies back on the mainland looking back on their vacations, reminiscing about their brief affairs with the lover who ruined all other men for them. It was hard work being a ladies' man, but Ashley was up for it. The notches on the bedposts of his king-size waterbed were evidence of his dedication to his craft.

He loved his gig at Edy's. There was a nonstop parade of hot pieces of ass passing through the place. And besides the plentiful tourist tail, there were also plenty of celebrities to hobnob with. Ashley liked getting near the rich and famous. He figured some of that glamor was bound to rub off on him. That's why he was sticking close to the SCSN film crew who were set up in the ocean view booth at the front of the restaurant. He'd never seen a live TV broadcast so up close and personal before. Even for a man of the world like himself, it was pretty damn exciting.

Jimmy John Jackson—Triple J himself—was seated at a table with Don Merryman and Billy "Blueshoes" Marvis, both of them runners-up for the Heisman trophy during their college careers and now Pro Bowlers for Dallas. It was cool stuff. Ashley wasn't the biggest football fan, but even a casual observer knew who these guys were.

He stationed himself just behind the camera, standing next to Whitey Andrews, the big

shot producer who had been hanging around Edy's for the past couple days. Ashley had watched him trying to seal the deal with Charlotte O'Daniel with steady determination and perseverance. He figured that made him and Whitey kindred spirits. Ashley had been down that road, enduring Charlotte's increasingly nasty rejections. The chick might as well have been wearing one of those chastity belts. Maybe Whitey, with all his connections to star power, might have better luck.

"Okay, everybody," Whitey called out. "We're going live, so let's have some quiet."

The chatter and clinking of plates and silverware ratcheted down a notch to a dull roar.

An assistant swooped in and gave Triple J's hair one final swipe of the comb, then disappeared into the background. Turning on his thousand-watt smile, Triple J grabbed his microphone and proceeded to charm the camera.

"Hey there, football fans, this is Jimmy John Jackson for the Southern Sports Network. I'm coming to you live from scenic Molokai, Hawaii as part of our ongoing coverage of the NFL's Paradise Week." He paused long enough for the camera to zoom out and show the guests seated on his right. "I'm here with a couple of Dallas Pro Bowlers, quarterback Billy 'Blueshoes' Marvis and his favorite receiving target, Don Merryman. How are liking Hawaii, fellas?"

The two football players mumbled something about enjoying the island hospitality then got back to slurping from hurricane glasses full of some electric blue concoction. Since

Michelle had taken the day off, Carla was subbing behind the bar. She regarded drink recipes as mere suggestions and got creative with ingredients. There was no telling exactly what was in those neon cocktails, but Ashley figured that it was mostly booze.

"Last year's first round playoff game was an instant classic," Triple J continued. "Dallas rallied from a three touchdown deficit and tied it up late in the fourth quarter. Then, with the clock running down, Blueshoes, you hooked up with Dapper Don Merryman for a forty yard touchdown that put the game on ice and punched your ticket to the playoffs."

Merryman and Marvis just nodded and kept drinking. Ashley had to stifle laughter. It was damn funny scene: a couple of big, scary black dudes wearing floral pattern shirts and flower leis while sipping bright blue tropical drinks. And there was Triple J, looking like he just stepped off the set of an aftershave commercial. There were a few beats of uncomfortable silence as Triple J came to the realization that no further answer was forthcoming. It looked like a double post pattern with a crossing route underneath to pick off the outside linebacker. You also had running back Clovis Jefferson on the wheel route, which froze the defensive end, drew in the free safety, and gave you a free shot at the endzone. That sound right?"

"Yup," Blueshoes said. "That sounds like it."

"Right on." Merryman nodded sagely.

"Was that the way coach drew it up or did you check into that one?" Triple J asked. "What was said in that huddle?"

Merryman whipped off his sunglasses, leaned forward on his elbows, and stared the camera down as he said, "It was like this, Triple J. I said, 'All you brothers run vertical and you big honkies on the line try to keep them defenders off Blueshoes back.' Then we snapped the ball and got that shit done."

This time, Ashley couldn't stop his laughter.

Triple J looked like he'd been caught with his pants down

and his wiener in the wind. "Fellas, I'm going to remind you that we're broadcasting live."

Blueshoes shrugged. "What can I say, Triple J? This here motherfucker is crazy, but he can catch whatever I throw at his black ass."

Whitey threw his hands in the air. He hissed at the cameraman. "Cut to commercial. Now!"

An assistant stepped in and announced, "And we're clear, folks."

Blueshoes and Merryman popped up out of their seats and headed for the bar, leaving Triple J stunned. He looked at Whitey mournfully and said, "I think they just killed our careers."

Whitey shook his fist in the air. "What the hell was in those drinks?"

"They sure as hell weren't Shirley Temples, huh?" Ashley slapped Whitey on the shoulder. "Speaking of drinks, why don't you head up to the bar and tell Carla to give you a couple on me? You look like you could use it."

Whitey muttered a reply, but Ashley was already headed for the front door. After a scene like that, he needed a cigarette. He slipped out the front door and pulled a pack of Winstons from his pocket. Leaning against the wall, he sparked up and took a long drag. He couldn't feel too bad for Triple J. A guy like that always landed on his feet. Still, the look on his face was priceless. Ashley was still laughing about it a couple minutes later when the Airstream RV pulled into the parking lot.

"What the hell?" He dropped his smoke in the ashcan by the front of the restaurant.

The Airstream's back door swung open, giving Ashley a tantalizing glimpse of a group of topless women sporting cat ear headbands.

"Shit, that's Max's Foxy Felines! I don't believe it!" Ashley was a fan of their calendar and their quarterly magazine.

Rowdy Abilene and his partner Jade stepped out. They

grabbed some luggage then bid farewell the topless beauties. Ashley sighed as Jade closed the door on them. Looked like Triple J wasn't the only guy who was born lucky.

The two agents made their way across the parking lot and greeted him. Rowdy asked if Edy was around.

Ashley shook his head. "Sorry, my man. The boss lady hasn't been here all day. But your gal pal Donna called. She wants you guys to head over to her place. You don't mind me saying, she sounded like she'd been through the wringer."

"What are you driving these days, Ashley?" Jade asked.

"Got me a brand spanking new Lincoln. Why?" Ashley knew what was coming, but he asked anyway.

"Because we need to borrow it," Rowdy said.

Ashley knew better than to argue. These guys were there for him when it came to fixing parking tickets and helping him skate on the small matters of some illegal gambling and forged concert tickets, so he owed them. He handed over the keys.

"It's parked around back," he said. "And a full tank of gas wouldn't hurt that car one bit, you dig?"

"Yeah, yeah," Rowdy called over his shoulder.

When Ashley stepped back inside, the mood with the TV people had flipped from funereal to fun. He grabbed Whitey, who was headed for the bar, and asked what was going on.

"What'd I miss, Whitey?"

"That whole segment never aired," the producer gushed. "Some lady was out walking her yorkie and she wasn't paying attention. The dog chewed through a couple of cables behind the broadcast truck, so the signal dropped. Can you believe it? Good luck for us."

"Bad luck for the dog, though."

"Yeah, well, you know how it is." Whitey shrugged. "Win some, lose some. Looks like

we'll be going live again just as soon as they switch out that cable. You know Muffy Fremont, that female golfer? She's dropping in for an interview in a couple hours."

Ashely sauntered over to Triple J, who was slumped behind the table, looking like he'd just been smacked by the boogeyman.

"Cheer up, Triple J," Ashley said, giving him a playful punch on the shoulder. "I hear you're getting to interview that golf broad, Muffy Fremont."

"Yeah, lucky me," Triple J replied. "That chick is so dumb she went home early to study for her pap test."

Donna was on the phone when Rowdy and Jade finally arrived. Taryn answered their knock at the front door and led them into the living room. She grabbed a couple beers from the fridge and handed them over. It was silly to be so excited over a couple male visitors—she wasn't some teenage schoolgirl, after all—but Taryn was out of practice. The terms of her WitSec agreement stated that she wouldn't entertain guests without Donna's presence, and then only after the agency had run a complete background check on them. Those terms didn't leave much wiggle room for a social life.

Rowdy and Jade took the couch while Taryn perched on the arm of one of the armchairs. The three of them sat there, seemingly unsure of who should speak first, while they listened to Donna patiently explain the snake situation to Glen Dickson.

"Right, I'll tell him," she said. "No...I fixed the phone myself..."

She looked over her shoulders and rolled her eyes dramatically.

"No, Glen, I've never been mistaken for a man," she continued. "Have you? Goodbye."

She hung up the phone and joined them in the living room, taking a seat on the armchair next to Taryn.

"Well, what's the story?" Taryn asked. "Is there an APB out on the killer snake?"

"Glen says the officers from Game and Fish are looking for it," Donna replied. "But the word from the health department is that the snake is so filled with toxins that it's likely to die within the next few days anyway."

"Well, then I say we let them handle it," Taryn suggested. "We got enough on our plate without beating the bushes for that stupid snake."

"You got that right," Donna agreed.

Rowdy took a pull off his beer, wiped his mouth with the back of his hand, and got right down to business. "Okay, enough about the snake. Let's talk about how we get Edy back. I just happen to have a plan. Dawn's the best time to execute it, so we have a little less than twelve hours to prepare. We can discuss details, but first I want to take a look at that video you shot this morning."

Donna nodded. "I got it set up in my bedroom. The VCR in there is better than this hunk of junk out here."

"Why don't you have a look at the tape," Jade said. "I'll be out here checking the weapons and filling Taryn in on her part in all this."

Donna put her arm around Taryn's shoulders. "You know, it's okay if you don't want to do this. You're still a civilian. This isn't your responsibility."

"What? No way I'm sitting this out." Taryn looked offended. She crossed her arms over her chest and said, "I'll be damned if I chicken out and let my friends down. I'm in. Absolutely."

"Right on!" Jade pumped his fist in the air.

Donna stood up and motioned for Rowdy to follow her down the hall and into her bedroom. She closed the door behind them, scooped the remote control off the TV stand, and sat on the edge of the bed.

"Taryn's pretty cool, huh?" Rowdy said, taking a seat next to her. He was close enough that their thighs touched. "And this cover ID that Uncle Sam gave you, it's not so bad either."

Donna smiled. "For a small-time smuggler, Glen Dickson

isn't the worst boss in the world. And since Taryn and I started working there, the legit part of the business is actually showing a profit."

"Nice work, Agent Hamilton."

Donna waved off the compliment and fired the remote control at the TV. The screen came to life in a snowstorm of static. She fired the remote again, this time at the VCR. The screen went blue for a split second then resolved into footage of the Frisbee player and Short Bus Sandra.

Rowdy watched a few seconds, then said, "That's Sonny McArthur. They call him Shades. He was a trigger-man for the Cardenas cartel until Pablo and Rodrigo got sent up the river. A real sadistic butcher, this guy. A cartel hit is usually a bloody spectacle, but Shades has a reputation for going overboard. He was one of the cartel's go-to hitters when they needed to make a point. Word is that he's dropped upwards of fifty bodies. He fled the country before the rest of the scumbags could get swept up by the narcos and found employment with Seth Romero. We like Shades for the murder of those two local cops."

Donna shuddered. "Sounds like a real charmer."

"Don't recognize the girl," Rowdy said. "You know her?"

"She's local," Donna explained. "Not sure how she got hooked up with this guy, but she's not involved in anything criminal. The only thing she's guilty of is being dumb."

"Yeah, she'd have to be pretty dumb if she's making nice with a guy like Shades."

Donna turned away from the TV and took Rowdy's hand. "So, did you know the extent of Romero's operation when you asked me to stay in California? I mean, did you know guys like Shades were hanging around?"

"I just didn't want you to get hurt." Rowdy met her gaze. "I care about you too much to risk losing you."

"You can't control my life," she said, leaning in even closer.

"I don't want to control your life."

"Well, what do you want?" she asked.

"To suck the polish right off your toes…"

That was all the invitation she needed. She pressed her lips against his, kissing him with such intensity that she felt his breath catch in his throat. When she finally pulled away, they were both gasping for air.

"I've missed you," he said.

"Oh yeah?" Donna put her hand on his knee and moved it up his thigh until she encountered what she was looking for. "I can tell."

"How about taking a closer look just to make sure." He brushed her hand aside and stood up. He unbuttoned and unzipped, and presented her with visual proof of how much he'd missed her.

"Now that's what I call hard evidence," she said, taking him in her hand.

Once she was sure she had his engine in high gear, she stripped off her clothes and lay back on the bed. She spread her legs, presenting herself for closer inspection.

"So, tell me what you're thinking," she said, running her fingers over her breasts. Her nipples hardened, the pink skin pebbling at the faint scratch of her nails.

"What do I think?" He eased himself on to the bed and between her thighs. "I think one man's dream is another man's lunch."

Donna closed her eyes as he kissed her breasts. Gradually, he worked his way down lower and lower until he reached his ultimate destination.

Taryn did her best to get some small talk going with Jade, but after a few minutes of half-assed attempts at conversation, she decided she needed a drink to break the ice. If there was one thing her Vegas days had taught her, it was that alcohol's reputation as a social lubricant was well-deserved. She asked Jade if she could offer him anything from the bar.

"I used to work at a bar in Las Vegas," she said. "So I know my way around a cocktail shaker. And since there's not much to do out here in the boonies, we keep that bar over in the corner pretty well stocked."

"Well, now that you mention it, a drink does sound pretty good." He pointed to his injured shoulder. "You know, for medicinal purposes. But better make it something light."

"Light? Well, we have some Sprite and I think there's probably a few cans of Tab hiding in the back of the fridge."

Jade laughed. "No, I mean vodka."

"Oh, yeah, I get it." Taryn crossed the room to the wet bar in the corner. She grabbed the bottle of Smirnoff and half-turned to show it to Jade. "How about a martini?"

He gave her a thumbs-up. "Just bring me that bottle and some lemon peel if you got it."

Taryn grabbed a lemon from the fruit bowl on the bar and used a knife to take off a few strips of peel. She grabbed a couple glasses and the ice bucket, then took the stuff back to Jade.

This time, she sat next to him on the couch.

"Okay, time to show you how I drink a martini," he said, taking the vodka and lemon peel. "Vodka, medium dry. Lemon peel."

"I think I got it so far," Taryn said.

Jade popped the lemon peel straight into his mouth and started chomping. Ignoring the ice and the glasses, he twisted the cap off the bottle of vodka and took a big gulp. He swished it around in his mouth, then swallowed.

"Now that's how it's done," he sighed.

Taryn laughed. "Hey, it works for me. Secret agents should do their own thing. You're like Charlie Chan, right?"

"*Si, senorita...*" Jade winked and passed the bottle to Taryn.

She did her best to repeat his martini process, but the

mouthful of vodka left her sputtering. "Good Lord, that is a stiff drink…"

Jade laughed. "Yeah, and it's not the only thing that's stiff in this house, if you know what I mean."

Taryn felt heat creep into her cheeks. She'd been trying to ignore the noises coming from the other side of the house, but they seemed to be growing louder by the second. Donna was either having the best sex of her life or undergoing some intense religious conversion. She was certainly invoking the name of God repeatedly. Rowdy was exactly quiet either. He yelped and grunted like a man doing hard physical labor.

"Yes, yes, yes!" Rowdy's voice was loud and clear. "Give it to me, baby! Oh, yeah!"

"You like that?" Donna replied, panting like she'd just run an all-out sprint. "You want some more of that?"

That was the last of the intelligible dialogue. After that, their voices devolved in moans, yelps, and what Taryn could only think of as barnyard vocalizations.

"It sounds like someone's being murdered in there," Jade said.

"Yeah," she agreed. "Either that or it's feeding time at the zoo."

They looked at one another, their eyes wide as they tried to stifle laughter. The animal sounds grew in intensity and volume. Even when Taryn was sure they'd reached a crescendo, they continued.

"You know what? Maybe I'll just turn on the stereo," Taryn said, passing the vodka bottle back to Jade. "You heard that new Whitesnake album?"

"Sounds good to me," Jade replied.

They made it through the entire album, from "Crying in the Rain" to "Don't Turn Away," before the animal noises coming from Donna's bedroom finally stopped. A few minutes later, Rowdy and Donna came back into the living room. Rowdy had that bleary, self-satisfied smile that Taryn knew all too well. And

Donna was sporting what Taryn liked to call "sex hair," her blonde curls tousled and messy. Both of them sighed contentedly as they sat on the couch.

"Must have been some video," Jade said. "What was it, a director's cut? You were back there for a while."

Rowdy smirked. "We stopped for a bite to eat."

"Yeah, well, maybe you shouldn't chew your food so loudly," Taryn said.

Chapter Ten

When Edy had gotten picked up for possession of a controlled substance, grand theft auto, and DWI, the agents assigned to her case had offered to drop the charges in exchange for her cooperation in an ongoing investigation into the drug trafficking operations involving the Friendly Isle. At the time, she thought it sounded like a pretty sweet deal. After all, she was already exposed to most of Molokai's sordid gossip on a daily basis. How hard could it be to listen just a bit more, to watch just a little closer? Her attorney hadn't been quite as enthusiastic. He'd cautioned her that there were certain dangers involved with being a confidential informant. But Edy had dismissed his concerns out of hand. She figured a clean slate was worth the risk.

Now, she was wondering if maybe she should have considered the government's offer more carefully. She'd had plenty of time to ponder her life choices since that psycho Seth Romero had dragged her into his house and tied her up.

She was confined to a dark room, her hands bound and connected to a rope hanging from the ceiling. Her feet were tied together at the ankles. They hadn't bothered with a gag, because, as Romero had gleefully reminded her, there was no one with in miles of the house. She could scream as much as she wanted.

And for a while, she had done just that. Alone in that room, she'd screamed until she could taste blood in the back of her throat. Then, with the full weight of hopelessness bearing down on her, she'd sagged to the floor. She closed her eyes and allowed herself a moment of self-pity, then shook it off. Edy St. James was not about to be broken by this gang of low-life criminals. She'd survived an abusive drunk of a father and two husbands cut from a similar cloth. She'd fended off unwanted advances from lecherous men, sometimes even resorting to violence to make her point. No matter how much she looked like a delicate flower, she could more than hold her own when push came to shove. And if this thing went south and took her to the end of the line? Well, she'd be damned if she would give them the satisfaction of wilting.

After a quiet interval—Edy didn't know if it was hours or minutes later—the door opened and three men entered the room. Romero came in first, followed by two others that she recognized as occasional patrons of Edy's Bar and Grill. The fat one was named Harry or Larry, something like that. The smaller one was Kimo. He'd dated several of the waitresses, showering them with gifts and affection until they put out, then moving on to another sucker. She could smell his cologne as soon as he entered the room.

Harry (or Larry) grabbed the rope and tugged her to her feet. Pacing back and forth in front of her, Romero peppered her with questions. Who was she working for? Where were the diamonds? How much did she know about his operation?

Edy knew better than to answer. Once they were sure they'd gotten all they could from her, they'd feed her to the sharks. As long as they thought there was something useful she could tell them, they'd keep her alive. Maybe she could hang around long enough to be rescued. Sooner or later, Rowdy and Jade would realize she wasn't coming to pick them up, and they'd start looking for her.

So she tried like hell to convince Romero that she didn't know anything. Even when Kimo put his switchblade against her throat, she steadfastly denied knowing anything about Romero or his operations.

"You're lying to me," he said, glaring at her. "You know something, and you're going to tell me what it is. Right now, I'm asking nicely, but my patience is wearing thin."

Edy recoiled. "Yeah, and your mouthwash gave up a long time ago."

He drew back his hand like he was going to slap her then stopped himself. He dropped his hand to his side and took a step back. He looked at his two subordinates.

"You know what, fellas?" His smile spread slowly, his lips pulling back to reveal his polished white teeth. "I think she needs an attitude adjustment. Rosie's good at that sort of thing."

"Yeah, she's one hell of a motivator," Kimo agreed. "I'll go get her."

Kimo pocketed his knife and left the room. The two remaining men just stared at her while they waited for him to return. It was unnerving. Edy felt like a race horse being scrutinized by a prospective buyer. She couldn't decide whether it was better to drop her gaze to the floor or to stare back at the two thugs.

The door to the room opened and Edy got another whiff of Kimo's cologne as he stepped inside. Following close behind him was another familiar face. Rosie was another patron of the restaurant, accompanying Romero whenever he stopped in for a meal.

When Rosie came to the restaurant, she was casually and conservatively attired. Even so, it was always apparent that she was no stranger to the weight room at the local gym. But there in Seth Romero's interrogation room, it was a different story.

Rosie's attire left no room for doubt about her physical conditioning. She wore a black bikini that revealed nearly every inch of her oiled-up, bulging muscles. She looked like she'd been chiseled from stone. The expression on her face had all the warmth and emotion of a granite slab. Her dead, unblinking eyes traveled over Edy, sizing her up slowly, from head to toe and back again. She held a pair of nunchaku at her side, tapping the black wooden sticks against her thigh as she stepped closer.

"Hello, Edy," she said. "It's nice to see you again. You look positively radiant, as always."

Edy sneered. "And you look like you stepped out of a bad comic book. What the hell are you supposed to be anyway?"

Rosie stepped to the middle of the room and struck a pose that was equal parts ballerina and bodybuilder. Her muscles bulged beneath her sun-bronzed skin.

"Yeah, I don't think I need to hang around for this part," Kimo said. He patted Rosie on the shoulder on his way out of the room. "Have fun, sis."

Rosie shifted to another pose, arching her back and flexing her arms over her head.

The two remaining men must have known what was coming, because they stepped away and put their backs to the wall on the opposite side of the room. Harry (or Larry) smiled and rubbed his hands together like a hungry teenager at an all-you-can-eat pizza buffet. Romero just stared impassively.

Rosie held the pose for a full minute, then relaxed into a normal stance. In a series of quick, decisive movements, she stripped off her bikini and let it fall to the floor. Edy couldn't help but stare. Rosie was an impressive specimen. Every inch of her was tanned and toned.

"You like what you see?" Rosie said. "Because we can be friends, you and me. All you have to do is answer a few questions. Then we can retire to my bedroom and get to know one another better. More intimately. If you're good enough, I bet I can persuade Seth to let me keep you as a pet."

"Dream on, bitch." Edy shook her head. "Even if I did swing that way, I wouldn't have anything to do with you."

Rosie laughed as she walked a slow circle around Edy. "I've heard that one before. Trust me, you'll come around in the end. Soft, pretty bitches like you always do."

She paused behind Edy, pressing her muscular body against Edy's back. She snaked one arm around Edy's midsection. Her breath was hot and moist as she sighed into Edy's ear. A hand as rough and hard as teak wood slipped inside Edy's blouse and massaged her breast. Rosie held Edy even closer. She wrapped her other arm around Edy and pressed the tip of the nunchaku against her crotch. Edy squeezed her legs together, but Rosie was too strong to be denied.

"How about it, sweetheart?" Rosie whispered, her lips grazing Edy's earlobe. "Feel like answering the man's questions or do you still want to do this the hard way?"

"Get the fuck off me!" Edy screamed.

"Okay," Rosie laughed. "If that's the way you want it…"

Abruptly, she sprang to the center of the room. She snapped her nunchaku in front of her, holding one stick in each hand, the chain connecting them drawn taut.

"Trust me, Edy," she said. "We're going to become intimately acquainted, whether you like it or not."

Before Edy could formulate a response, Rosie burst into a complex routine that was part martial arts exhibition and part exotic dance. Her nunchaku became a blur as she swung them about her, tossing them from hand to hand as she moved. It was hypnotic. If Edy wasn't terrified out of her mind, she might have been impressed by the display. Then, the whirling nunchaku caught her in the stomach. The strike was so sudden and unexpected that it caught Edy off guard. The force of the blow drove the air from her lungs, and she doubled over in pain. Rosie grabbed a handful of her hair and hauled her back upright.

"How about now, cutie?" Rosie asked, letting go of her hair. "Ready to talk?"

Edy shook her head.

This time, it was Rosie's fist that slammed into Edy's stomach. It felt like a

sledgehammer. Edy gagged and sputtered, doubling over again. Rosie moved behind her and spanked her with the nunchaku. One, two, three sharp strikes of hardened wood to Edy's buttocks.

"You've been a bad girl, Edy," Rosie said, circling back in front of her. She shoved Edy to the floor and loomed over her. "Now, I'm going to let you sit here and weigh your options. When I come back, you can talk to me and then we'll go soak those bruises in a hot bath. Big bad Rosie will kiss them all better. Or you can continue to be a stubborn bitch and I'll give you a spanking that will make that one look like a sensual massage."

Edy closed her eyes and wished that Rowdy and Jade would hurry up.

As much as Seth Romero usually enjoyed Rosie's show, he was too preoccupied at the moment to be aroused by the display. Normally, he was glad when someone decided to play hard to get and Rosie had to really earn her keep, but right then, he would have loved it if Edy would just give up the goods.

He told Harry to keep an eye on Edy, then motioned for Rosie to follow him out of the room. They went down the hall to the room he'd converted to an office. He kept a bottle of Wild Turkey on his desk and he poured a couple inches into two glasses. He passed one of them to Rosie and drank the other in one gulp. He poured himself another round and sat down heavily behind his desk.

"Maybe she doesn't know anything after all," he sighed.

Rosie sat on the edge of the desk. "If I didn't know better, I'd say you felt sorry for that weak bitch. Michael heard her talking to those feds. She's just playing hardball. But don't you worry, I'll have her singing soon enough."

She drank her measure of bourbon then set the glass aside. She slipped off the desk and moved behind his chair.

"You're so tense," she said, kneading his shoulder muscles. "I can take care of that, you know. Want me to get my special outfit and the Vaseline?"

He shrugged her off. "This isn't the time for that. I'm supposed to call Mr. Chang and right now, I have no good news for him. Get out of here."

Rosie's shoulders sagged as she crossed the room. She opened the door, then paused and said, "You know, you can be a real asshole sometimes."

"Put on some fucking clothes," he growled.

She sniffed like she had something more to say, but then thought better of it and left the room, slamming the door behind her.

"Dirty pervert," Seth whispered, pouring himself another drink.

He felt bad about the remark, even if no one else was around to hear it. Rosie was his best employee, after all. He trusted her implicitly, both as his bodyguard and his lover. The latter was even harder to come by than the former, especially for someone with as many offbeat proclivities as Seth. Sure, it was easy enough to find some escort who was willing to dress up like a cavewoman and howl like a she-wolf while she rubbed her feet on his Vaseline-coated manhood, but the act would be entirely transactional. There'd be no enthusiasm for it. Rosie actually enjoyed that sort of thing, and that made all the difference. She was one in a million. Hell, maybe even better than that. Still, there was serious trouble afoot, and he needed her to get her head back in the game. There would be plenty of time for hanky-panky once he had his diamonds and these fucking feds weren't sniffing around.

He bolted down his drink and glanced at his Rolex. Time to call the boss. Seth hated

these phone calls. They only served to remind him that while he may have been the top dog in the Hawaii operation, he still had to answer to someone. He'd never been good at accepting authority. But he contented himself with the knowledge that sooner or later, everyone answered to someone. The food chain went on and on, and he couldn't even imagine where it might end. With God, he supposed. And even that didn't sit quite right with Seth. But these were philosophical problems, and he had more immediate concerns.

He snatched the desk phone off its cradle and dialed the number for Mr. Chang's Honolulu office. It was a direct line, so there was no secretary to contend with. Mr. Chang himself answered on the second ring.

"Mr. Romero, how nice of you to call." The voice was as gentle as a spring breeze. The British accent conveyed a sense of refinement and sophistication that intimidated Seth far more than any threat of violence.

"Yes, Mr. Chang. Yes, sir," Seth sputtered.

"I trust your payment arrived safely. We require another shipment of your product," Mr. Chang continued. "As you know, I take care to ensure that all my transactions are carried out with the utmost care and efficiency. I wish it were so for all of my business associates. Apropos of that wish, I should mention that your last shipment was, in fact, two kilos short."

"I'll see that he corrects the problem," Seth said. "Or the next delivery will include his head in a bag."

"Oh? And will this next shipment arrive on time or will it be late like the last one?"

"Yes, sir, I apologize for that. Relocating to the new property wasn't as smooth as I hoped. The former owners were very difficult to persuade. Production is back to our usual levels now, and we'll be right on schedule for the next shipment." Seth hated the sound of his voice during these calls. He was Seth Romero, after all. His reputation stretched from Miami to Honolulu. He shouldn't sound like a scolded child explaining himself to a stern parent.

"And I hear there is a small matter of federal agents. Feel free to correct me if my sources are incorrect," Mr. Chang continued.

Seth swallowed. Despite the drinks, his throat was suddenly dry. "Your sources are correct, but I'm handling that problem personally. I'll take care of those agents."

"See that you do, Mr. Romero. This interference cannot be allowed to continue. And make sure to do a thorough job. Show them no mercy, you understand? Let them witness the full power of our organization. Kill them all."

"I understand, sir."

The line went dead. Seth dropped the receiver back on its cradle.

He pushed his chair back from the desk and stood, rolling his head around on his shoulders. Rosie was right; he *was* tense. He thought about knocking back a few more drinks. Maybe getting a little loaded would do the trick. But he knew that was a bad idea. When he was drunk, there was no telling what he might do. He paced back and forth across the room, clenching and unclenching his fists. Finally, he came to a decision.

He strode out of the office and down the hall. He entered Rosie's room without knocking. His breath caught in his throat when he saw her. She stood in the middle of the room, wearing her cavewoman outfit: cheetah-print singlet that exposed one breast. Her hair had been teased into a wild riot of tangles. Her face was smeared with streaks of black and brown makeup to simulate dirt and grime.

He looked at her with undisguised hunger as he undressed.

"I knew you'd change your mind," she said, beckoning him toward her.

He glanced down at her feet then over to the nightstand, atop which an extra-large jar of petroleum jelly sat ready for use.

The snake's metabolism had reached an even higher gear. Already, its digestive system had begun to break down the pieces of the honeymooners that it had ingested. In a matter of hours, it had gone from sated and sluggish to fully alert, even hungry. Slithering through the dense undergrowth, back to the crawlspace beneath the house, the snake began to dream about its next meal.

But there was something else driving it forward. Something more potent and primitive that apex predator hunger. The snake no longer saw the kill as a means of survival, but as an end itself. Even if hunger was no longer a motivation, the snake's bloodlust would remain. It wanted to revel in violence and death. It wanted to kill and kill and kill until the bodies of its victims were heaped before it like a reeking, decaying mountain. It wanted to swim in rivers of blood. It wanted to fill its lair with the sun-bleached bones of its prey.

By the time it reached the house and squeezed into the dark crawlspace, the snake was temporarily exhausted. It had traveled miles through tangles of weeds and vines, over rocks and twisted tree roots. The muscles beneath its sleek hide ached. It slithered into a corner and coiled upon itself. The sound of water rushing through the pipes overhead lulled it to sleep, and it dreamed blood-drenched visions of death and decay.

They cleared away the coffee table and sat in a circle on the living room floor with the cache of weapons spread out on the carpet. Donna had to admit that it was quite an arsenal. Nobody could ever accuse Rowdy and Jade of traveling light. A lot of it was the usual stuff: 9mm pistols, riot-police style shotguns, and plenty of ammunition. There were some more exotic pieces of hardware as well. A pair of Uzi submachine guns confiscated from the Central American drug cartels, a box of flash-bang grenades, and a crossbow that fired wicked steel tipped bolts. It was an impressive array of firepower, but nothing too out of the ordinary, apart from that crossbow and the four-barreled monstrosity that Rowdy called his "shoulder canon."

"It fires rocket propelled grenades," Rowdy explained, running his fingers over the flat black surface of the boxy weapon. "It's a prototype, so this baby is one of a kind. Basically, it's a scaled down version of an anti-tank weapon. Lightweight, easy to load, and almost zero recoil. Shoot this baby at someone, and they're nothing but a distant memory."

"Wow," Taryn said. "That's cool!"

Jade laughed. "He's leaving out the part about how it's pretty much the only thing he can use to actually hit a target."

Donna patted Rowdy's thigh. "It's okay, baby. Your marksmanship doesn't define you as a man."

After they finished laughing, they got down to business cleaning and loading the weapons. It was a repetitive, mindless activity, but Donna actually liked that. It helped her clear her mind. Even with Taryn's constant chatter, there was a certain meditative quality to the process. She was so wrapped up in getting her own hardware ready that she didn't notice Rowdy's current project until he was nearly finished with it. Brow wrinkled with concentration, he was busy slotting two-inch serrated blades into the edges of a black Frisbee.

"I think this little beauty is ready for action," he said, holding up the improvised weapon.

"What the hell is that?" she asked.

He inserted the final blade and held up the disc for her inspection. He wore a pair of black gloves lined with steel mesh, the kind of gloves used for shucking oysters. A self-satisfied smile spread across his face. "Just a little surprise I've been preparing for our friend Shades."

"Yeah, a deadly surprise," Jade added. "Those blades are so sharp, they'll cut your eyeballs open if you look at them too long."

Handling it by the edges, Rowdy tucked the improvised weapon into a canvas satchel.

"Hey, Donna," he said. "You still got that little ultralight?"

The item in question was a 220-pound rotorcraft that she'd used during her early days as a field agent. It wasn't the most practical vehicle for law enforcement, so it had mostly ended up as a way to kill boredom while she was still in the process of getting her pilot's license.

She nodded. "Sure. Doesn't get much use these days now that I have the Cessna, but it's out there in the garage. Why?"

He smiled. "Because I think what this rescue operation needs is air support. Tomorrow morning, we kick ass and take names."

"I like the sound of that," Taryn said.

"Well, then listen up," Rowdy continued. "Here's the plan, ladies and gentlemen..."

Chapter Eleven

Rowdy parked the Jeep at the trailhead. He told Jade and Taryn to hang back until he'd finished his business with Shades.

"I don't understand," Taryn said. "We have every type of gun you could want. Why don't we just shoot this guy?"

"It's personal between me and this asshole," Rowdy explained. "A few years ago, when I was working the Colombian cocaine pipeline, my unit had an informant in the Cardenas cartel. She'd been relaying information to the agency for a little over a year. Nothing much, just the location of some smaller drops, the names of some of the low level dealers. She was just a bartender in Rodrigo Cardenas' strip club in Cartagena. Somehow, her cover got blown. Her wire went dead, and two weeks later, the Colombian police found what was left of her in a dumpster behind a dog-fighting club."

"Jesus," Taryn gasped. "You mean that this Shades dude is the one that did it?"

"A separate wiretap caught him bragging about it to one of his lackeys," Rowdy said, climbing out of the Jeep. "He could hardly stop laughing while he laid out the gory details."

He grabbed his canvas satchel from the backseat and slipped

the strap over his shoulder. Inside the bag was the weaponized Frisbee, a nine-millimeter pistol, a walkie-talkie, and a change of clothes. His current attire—shorts and a t-shirt—fit the bill of a disc-throwing beach bum, but he'd need something more substantial once they made their move on Romero's house.

"Her name was Mariposa Flores," Rowdy said. "She was only twenty-three years old, and Shades butchered her and left her for dog food. It's time he faced justice."

"Go get that son of a bitch," Jade said, his face uncharacteristically grave.

Rowdy took a deep breath and headed for the beach. The sun was barely above the blue line of the horizon. By now, Sandra would be out for her morning stroll along the beach, followed by a friendly Frisbee match with Shades. The weather was perfect for it, after all. The breeze was just enough to be pleasantly refreshing, but too light to throw off a flying disc's trajectory.

Rowdy caught up to her about a half-mile from her usual Frisbee spot. She was wearing a pair of cut-off jeans and a bright yellow tank top emblazoned with a smiley face. She giggled each time the edge of the surf washed up far enough to tickle her toes. She held a black Frisbee in her hand.

"Hey, there," Rowdy called, trotting up alongside her. "Nice morning, huh?"

She smiled. "Sure is."

Rowdy introduced himself, offering his hand to shake.

"My name's Sandra. Nice to meet you." She slapped him five in lieu of the handshake, giggling like she'd just remembered some private joke.

"Mind if I tag along?" Rowdy asked.

"It's a free country," she said. "And besides, you're cute."

Rowdy could instantly tell that Donna hadn't understated Sandra's lack of intelligence. She had that "lights are on but nobody's home" look. It was a good thing nature had blessed her with head full of strawberry blonde curls, a smile worthy of a toothpaste commercial, and a body made for a bikini, because it was clear Sandra wasn't going to wow anyone with her conversational skills.

"Hey, this may sound like a random question," Rowdy said, "but you wouldn't happen to know anyone around here who might be up for throwing the old Frisbee around, would you? See, none of my friends are any good with a disc, and I'm trying to keep my skills sharp while I'm on vacation. And I noticed you have a Frisbee, so I figured…"

"Oh, wow, man. That's not random at all," Sandra gushed. "There's this guy I meet up with most mornings, and we throw the Frisbee around for a while. I'm not so good at it, but he can really zip that thing around and do all these fancy tricks. If you want, I'll introduce you."

"That'd be awesome!" Rowdy said.

For the rest of their walk, Sandra kept up a stream of consciousness monologue about everything from her job (waitress at a breakfast restaurant) to her views on illegal aliens (she thought they should stay in their flying saucers) to the new Rick Astley single (she just knew people would still be singing along to it forty years down the road). Rowdy wondered if she had superhuman lung capacity that allowed her to say so much without ever taking a breath.

"Oh, hey, there he is," she said, pointing ahead. "See him? He's the guy with the blonde hair and the sunglasses. He, like, always wears those shades. They look like cop glasses to me. You think he might be a cop? 'Cause he usually carries a gun too. Kinda weird to carry that around if you're not a cop, huh?"

As they approached, Shades made his displeasure known.

"What the hell, Sandra?" he asked, putting a hand on the butt of the gun holstered on his hip. "You just show up with some guy? Who is that turkey, anyway? Looks like he's carrying a purse."

"Oh, relax, would you?" Sandra rolled her eyes. "He's just a guy looking to throw the Frisbee. And besides, I read in a magazine that men in Europe carry purses all the time."

"Well, beat it, buster," Shades said, jabbing a finger in Rowdy's direction. "You ain't allowed here."

"Come on," Sandra pleaded. "Don't be such a butthole. This guy says he's a pretty good thrower."

"Oh yeah?" Shades sneered. He looked like he'd taken a bite of something sour. "We'll just see about that."

Sandra passed her red disc to Rowdy. She bounced on her feet and clapped her hands. "Oh, dude, this is, like, so exciting!"

Rowdy whipped the disc at Shades, who snatched it out of the air. He spun it on one finger, did a nifty between-the-legs move, then sent it flying back.

Rowdy grabbed the disc out one-handed. He fired it back, this time putting a little extra heat on it. Shades spun around and caught it behind his back. Showing off, he did the between-the-legs thing again. He flung it back at Rowdy, even harder this time. Rowdy nearly caught one in the face, but he managed to make the grab before the disc screwed with his dental work.

"A little too hot for you to handle?" Shades snickered.

Rowdy drew back his arm and returned service. The throw was off the mark, sailing over Shades' head into the trees lining the inland edge of the beach.

"Nice one, asshole." Shades trotted off to retrieve the disc.

Once Shades was out of sight, Rowdy grabbed Sandra by the arm.

"Baby, I think it's time for you to leave," he said, lifting his shirttail to show her the gun in his waistband. "Things are about to heat up here."

She may not have been a deep thinker, but Sandra knew better than to hang around. She nodded. "Yeah, I think you're right."

She turned to run away, but Rowdy reeled her back in. He

planted a kiss on her cheek and said, "You know something? You've got a great ass. Just thought you should know."

Sandra giggled. "So do you, pilgrim."

She turned and bounded away, leaving footprints in the wet sand as she skipped down the beach, singing to herself.

"Hey, where's she going?" Shades called as he jogged out of the trees, disc in hand.

Rowdy shrugged. "Must have a hot date."

"Yeah, whatever." Shades drew back his arm. "See if you can catch this, pretty boy."

Rowdy managed to make the grab, surprising himself in the process. He figured it was a sign from the universe that it was time to make his move. He dropped the disc and shook his hand, feigning an injury.

"Oh, come on, Mr. European Purse." Shades threw back his head and laughed. "It wasn't that hard of a throw. Don't be such a Nancy."

Rowdy turned around and crouched to retrieve the disc. He lifted the flap on his satchel and exchanged the normal disc for the deadly one, taking care to grip it between the blades.

"This is for Mariposa and the Molokai cops," he muttered as he stood.

"Come on, quit stalling," Shades said.

Rowdy turned and threw the disc in one fluid motion. He knew as soon as it left his hand that it was right on the money. Strangely enough, being such a poor marksman had given him a feel for when something was on target. It was such a rare sensation that it was almost electric.

Shades raised his right hand to make the catch. The blades, spinning like a circular saw, cut through his fingers, snipping all four off like garden shears through rose stems. The deadly disc's speed and trajectory weren't much affected. It spun onward, ripping into Shades' neck, severing his jugular and embedding itself in his throat. The disc stuck there. Shades raised his ruined hand and pawed uselessly at it. Blood jetted from the stumps of his fingers. More blood poured from his severed veins and arteries, running over the disc. He tried again, this time with his uninjured hand. All he succeeded in doing was losing a few more fingers and a lot more blood. Fat droplets pattered on the sand. He opened his mouth and gagged out a series of wet gurgling noises. Finally, he collapsed.

Rowdy had seen enough violent deaths to know that Shades was likely dead before his head lolled back on the sun-warmed sand. It was lights out for that psychopath.

"Gotcha," Rowdy said, looking down at the dead hitman. He allowed himself a few seconds to celebrate the victory then dug his walkie-talkie out of his satchel. He thumbed the button and, after a brief squall of static, said, "Okay, guys, it's a beautiful day on the beach. Come on down. And Donna? The skies are clear for takeoff."

Nobody was ever going to mistake the Cessna for a fighter jet, but compared to the ultralight, it was like something out of *Top Gun*. It was like comparing a tractor to a weed whacker: yes, they basically accomplished the same thing, broadly speaking, but there were considerable differences in size and power.

Donna had forgotten how relatively quiet the ultralight's engine was, how thin and insubstantial its frame was. She felt like she might drop out of the sky at any moment. Still, Rowdy was right. It was a beautiful day on the beach. And besides, the old familiar tingle of impending action was starting to spread throughout her body. Once the action got cranked up, that pleasant sensation would intensify until it bordered on erotic. No doubt about it, Donna Hamilton was built for the life of a field agent.

She took the ultralight in low, circling the house once to get her bearings.

"All right, guys," she said into her headset radio. "It's time to light these sons of bitches up. Bombs away!"

The flash-bang grenades were strapped across her chest like a bandolier. There were six of them, which might have been considered overkill, but they wanted to draw the attention of Romero's goons away from the main part of the house. Nothing like fire from above for making an impression.

She tugged one of the grenades free, pulling the pin in the process. She lobbed it underhand, watching it bounce on the front lawn before exploding in a white-hot flash. Even from Donna's altitude, the concussion was thunderous. Donna smiled. She felt like some ancient goddess hurling thunderbolts at the earth.

Below her, the Jeep had arrived. It skidded to a halt just outside the retaining wall that ringed the front yard. Taryn, Rowdy, and Jade wore air traffic controller-style ear protectors and dark sunglasses to protect them from the noise and flash of the grenades. They jumped out of the Jeep with weapons at the ready and spread out as they advanced on the house. So far, everything was proceeding according to plan. She really had to hand it to Rowdy. He was as skilled a tactician as he was deficient as a marksman.

Donna circled the house again and dropped another grenade. Before this one detonated, she'd already tossed two more. By now, Romero's mercenary army was streaming out of the house on all sides. She dropped one of the remaining grenades, then laughed as they stumbled around the yard, disoriented by the explosions. She tossed the last grenade then headed back down the beach, where there was enough open space to land the ultralight. It didn't feel right, leaving the others behind, but there was just no safe way to land the aircraft at the estate, not with that helicopter taking up so much of the front yard. She'd have to go back to the trailhead parking lot. She just hoped the fighting wouldn't be over before she could make it back to the Daioo estate.

The adrenaline rush of a free-fire operation didn't sharpen Rowdy's aim one bit. In fact, all the excitement might have actually made it worse. When it came to marksmanship as bad as his, it was really hard to discern degrees of inaccuracy. Even with his rifle on full auto, rocking and rolling to the tune of five rounds per second, he couldn't manage a single bullseye. One would think that a few bullets would find their mark, if only because the law of averages would kick in. But that wasn't the case at all.

Still, the enemy didn't know he'd failed every single marksmanship class he'd ever taken, and they ran for cover as he fired. As a result, their return fire was just as wild as his, and for the first few seconds of the engagement, both sides only succeeded in making one hell of a racket as they wasted bucket loads of ammo.

Rowdy took cover behind the retaining wall as bullets whizzed overhead. Jade fell in beside him, pausing to eject a spent magazine from his AK-47 and replace it with a fresh one.

"Tell me the truth," Jade said. "You're not really this bad of a shot, are you? Missing every target with such consistency has to be intentional."

Rowdy gave him a look. He chose not to dignify the remark with a response, and instead, asked where Taryn was.

Jade nodded in the direction of the house. "She's flanking them, going around that sun room to catch them from behind. By the time Donna gets here, we'll have them in the kill box for sure."

"I like all that tough guy talk," Rowdy said. "Gets me all hot and bothered."

"Okay, then try this one on for size," Jade replied. "Let's kill some bad guys and rescue the girl."

Taryn thought it was a shame that a scumbag like Seth Romero had taken over the Daioo estate. Even by the standards of the island's wealthy citizens, the house was beautiful. Of course, the beachfront side was currently hosting a spirited firefight as Jade and Rowdy shot it out with Romero's thugs. That gorgeous stucco and natural stone exterior was going to need plenty of repairs when this day was over.

The entire east side of the house was taken up by one large sunroom. It was the sort of thing Taryn had seen in magazines. It was almost enough to move her to tears when she fired a quick burst of bullets at the sunroom's door, reducing the frosted glass to a pile of jagged shards. She supposed that was just how it went. Couldn't make an omelet without breaking eggs, just like you couldn't execute a rescue mission without massive destruction of property.

She stepped into the tastefully decorated room, checking for any gunmen who might be lurking in the corners. It appeared that she was alone.

Maybe this secret agent shit isn't so hard after all, she thought.

The sigh of relief had just escaped her lips when the bullet whizzed by her head and shattered one of the glass walls behind her. She dove into the space between the sofa and grand piano. She paused just long enough to catch her breath then sprang up, sweeping the barrel of her Uzi in a wide arc as she emptied the magazine.

Her assailant fled through the shattered doorway, running into the side yard and vaulting over the retaining wall. Taryn saw just enough to recognize him as the bartender from Edy's. Hard to believe that nerdy guy with the Coke bottle glasses and receding hairline was also Michelle. Even harder to believe he was some hardened criminal.

Guess you just never really know with some people, Taryn thought.

She ejected the empty magazine and reloaded with practiced

ease. All the firearms lessons Donna had drilled into her were finally paying off. Her boots crunched bits of broken glass as she crossed the room.

The Guy Also Known as Michelle popped up from the behind the stone wall like a pissed off jack-in-the-box. He snapped off two shots with his pistol, but Taryn danced out of the line of fire. Two more of the floor-to-ceiling windows shattered.

"Missed me, asshole!" Taryn shouted.

She returned fire, clipping him in the right forearm. His scream was high and girlish, sounding more appropriate for his alter ego. The gun flew from his hand, coming to rest on the other side of the wall. Still shrieking, he dove across the stone barrier and made a grab for it with his left hand. Taryn ducked behind the slender trunk of a palm tree, hoping that he couldn't shoot very well left-handed. She closed her eyes, bracing herself and hoping the tree was enough to absorb the bullets. But nothing happened.

She peeked out from behind the tree and saw the Guy Also Known as Michelle furiously squeezing the trigger of a gun that was completely out of ammunition. He locked eyes with her for a second, growling in frustration as the hammer of his gun clicked on an empty chamber again.

"You know what?" Taryn said, raising her own gun and taking careful aim. "Edy should have fired your ass a long time ago. Who the hell tends bar in a classy joint and makes such a shitty martini?"

She didn't allow the bartender the opportunity for an excuse. The Uzi jumped in her hands, rattling off a staccato riff of gunfire. The Guy Also Known as Michelle went down in a hail of bullets, his final breath coming out choked with blood.

Taryn stood there for a moment, not quite knowing how to feel. She'd never gunned someone down before. Since she'd decided to start training for a job with the agency, she'd played the scenario out in her imagination dozens of times. She knew there was strong possibility that a job as a field agent would require her to use lethal force. She just didn't expect it to come so soon.

A hand came down on her shoulder and she yelped. She spun around with her gun raised, but that same hand caught the barrel of the Uzi and pushed it away.

"Donna!" Taryn sighed with relief at the sight of her roommate and mentor. "I was hoping you'd make it back soon."

Donna was armed with the crossbow she'd taken from Rowdy's arsenal. To Taryn, she looked like some superhero getting ready to save the world.

"Looks like you wasted your first bad guy," Donna said, nodding toward the corpse.

Taryn shrugged. "Yeah, I guess so."

"We'll talk it out later," Donna said. "But right now, we have more pressing business. Rowdy and Jade are going in, so we need to cover the exterior of the house. You up for shooting more scumbags if necessary?"

Taryn smiled, hefting the Uzi. "Just let those bastards try to get past me."

Jade crept through the house with all the stealth of a jungle cat stalking its prey. His soft-soled boots were barely a whisper on the plush carpet as he moved from room to room. The place seemed empty. He hoped they hadn't moved Edy to another location. It would be one hell of a bummer to find out this whole mission might have been for nothing. Of course, they'd done plenty of damage to Romero's operation regardless of whether or not they achieved their primary objective. He and Rowdy had cut a bloody swath through Romero's army of mercenaries and assassins. Romero's fighting capability had been greatly reduced.

Jade almost laughed. His internal monologue sounded like one of the instructors back at the academy. Back in those days, his brain had soaked up that tactical jargon like a sponge. A few years later, while on his first undercover assignment, he'd discovered the writings of Miyamoto Musashi and Sun Tzu. After that, a bunch of tactical vocabulary just seemed like gobbledygook from the mouths of men who'd lost touch with the spiritual nature of the warrior.

Jade paused at the end of a hallway. He closed his eyes and took a deep breath, shrugging off his preconceived notions of being a federal agent and looking inward to his spiritual core. Tranquility washed over him. Advancing with the same deadly silence, he moved down the hallway, checking the first room he encountered. It was a bedroom, and judging by the state of it, one that had seen recent use. The sheets and blankets on the king size bed were tangled and twisted. A large container of Vaseline and a studded dog collar sat on the nightstand.

"Someone's been naughty," Jade murmured, moving back into the hallway.

He checked two more bedrooms, neither of which were nearly as amusing as the first. Then he stepped into a larger, mostly empty room with a beautiful hardwood floor and walls adorned with Japanese *Ukiyo-e* art prints. Between the paintings were wooden racks holding various martial arts weapons: katana, nunchaku, and others. Jade whistled appreciatively. He walked to the center of the room to get a closer look. No doubt about it, whoever was responsible for this décor was on a wavelength similar to his own. The apartment he rented back in California was standard issue stuff. No way his landlord would allow him to convert the space into a dojo. Still, a guy could dream.

"Someone has good taste," he said, stepping closer to a wall to examine a print of Hokusai's *The Great Wave of Kanagawa*.

He was so wrapped up in his art appreciation that he didn't hear the person enter the room until it was almost too late. The whisper-soft footsteps were barely audible until the assailant was only a few feet from Jade. But that was still enough time for Jade to slip into combat mode and duck the spinning heel kick that was aimed at his head. He hit the floor, tucking and rolling away from the attack. He sprang to his feet, instantly assuming a defensive posture as he took stock of his attacker.

The Asian man standing across from him was obviously athletic, and judging by the ease with which he cycled through a serious of martial arts stances, an expert in several fighting styles. He was barefoot and dressed in a black karate *gi*. His hair was meticulously feathered, and the sides of his mustache drooped below his bottom lip. Jade had to admit it, this dude had style.

"What are you, Romero's personal ninja?" Jade asked. "Must be desperate times if you're working for that asshole."

"Whatever you say, *gaijin*," the man answered, throwing a series of punches at the air between them.

"Well…" Jade removed his shirt and flexed his muscles. His wounded shoulder still ached, but the first trickles of fight adrenaline were beginning to override his sense of pain. "It just so happens I know a thing or two about kung fu fighting myself, short stuff."

The ninja-for-hire laughed. "Did you take a free lesson at the YMCA? Bring it on, then. You don't scare me."

"Life's a bitch," Jade said, "and then you die."

He knew from experience never to judge a fighter by his size, but the barb was intended to throw the opposition off his game. A fighter who'd lost his sense of combat tranquility was much easier to defeat. He opened his mouth to spout another insult, but the ninja-for-hire had apparently heard enough and launched an opening salvo of punches that Jade blocked with ease. The roundhouse kick was another matter. The ninja's heel caught Jade in the ribs and sent him staggering a few steps back. A second kick smacked him in the face, opening a cut on his bottom lip. The ninja danced away, striking a few poses to taunt his opponent.

"I learned that from my sensei Karogawa," the ninja said.

"Not bad," Jade said, spitting blood onto the polished wood floor. "Now it's my turn."

The ninja tried for a third kick, but Jade caught his foot before it could connect. Then he landed a kick of his own, right to the ninja's balls.

"I learned that from my older sister Tracy," Jade said.

The ninja recovered from his coughing fit and threw a flurry of punches at Jade's midsection. Jade dropped his elbows and blocked most of them. He sidestepped the ninja's next attack and dealt him an open-handed slap to the face.

"And my first girlfriend Amanda taught me that one when I got too fresh at the homecoming dance." Jade was starting to enjoy this. "She could probably kick your ass without breaking a sweat."

That enjoyment was short-lived when the ninja sprang towards the weapons rack and grabbed a pair of nunchaku. If weapons were entering the equation, the stakes were raised. The ninja twirled and spun the nunchaku until they were a blur, then came straight at him. Jade had to use every evasive trick in the book to avoid getting his clock cleaned. He dove for the floor and tucked at the last split second, rolling out of harm's way. The ninja's momentum carried him past Jade, who used the opening to land a kick to his backside. Howling indignantly, the ninja crashed to the floor, nunchaku flying from his hand and clattering across the floor. Strolling past the weapons rack, Jade grabbed a pair of *shuko*, the dreaded ninja tiger claws. They looked like fingerless gloves with five hooked blades attached to the underside. For close fighting, they were a vicious, deadly weapon.

The *shuko* were a tight fit, but Jade managed to work them onto his hands before the ninja could gather himself and mount another attack. For the first time in the fight, Jade was going on the offensive.

The ninja employed some low kicks to keep Jade from closing in, but Jade could be a patient fighter when he needed to be. He returned fire in the form of some open-handed strikes that whiffed just past the ninja's face. Then, just as the ninja extended himself with a higher kick, Jade slipped away, circling behind the ninja and pulling him into a bear hug.

"Checkmate, dickhead," Jade laughed.

The ninja glanced down, seeming to notice the *shuko* for the first time. Before he could wriggle away, the cruel tips of the metal claws dug into his neck.

"These hands are deadly weapons," Jade whispered into the ninja's ear.

He gripped the ninja's neck tighter and tighter until all of the metal claws were embedded in the ninja's throat. Hot blood squelched through Jade's fingers.

"Life's a bitch…" Jade said.

The ninja gagged and gurgled. He clawed at Jade's hands, but the death grip only tightened. Finally, the ninja sagged, nothing but dead weight. Jade dropped the lifeless body to the floor.

"And then you die," Jade pronounced, looming over the dead ninja.

Kimo limped through the backyard, leaving a trail of blood on the bright green, meticulously maintained lawn. He scrabbled over the retaining wall and sat down heavily on the ground, nearly screaming as his wounded backside made contact with the ground. He leaned to his left, shifting his weight to his unharmed ass cheek.

He sat there for a moment with his eyes closed, breathing heavily and bleeding. His body throbbed with pain. Everything between his neck and ankles felt like it was on fire. Each breath felt like it was breaking his ribs on the way in and out.

Once his pulse had calmed a bit, he opened his eyes and surveyed the damage. It wasn't pretty.

He'd been up front when the feds first arrived and had joined in the firefight. At first, it hadn't been so bad. One of the feds had such bad aim he couldn't have hit the broadside of a cruise ship, even with his hotshot automatic weapon. And one of them was a girl, for crying out loud. Not a girl like Rosie, either, but a soft, pretty chick with blonde hair and big tits. Call him sexist or old-fashioned, but Kimo just couldn't accept that a chick who looked like she stepped out of a music video could be a real threat. And that was probably Kimo was in the shape he was in. He'd gotten cocky. Underestimating the strength of the opposition was a mistake. In all the noise and confusion, he'd been wounded not once or twice, but five times.

"Fucking fuckers shot me," he moaned, wincing as he checked his injuries.

Two of the shots had caught him in the right shoulder. One had passed through, but the other had smashed his collarbone. He supposed that bullet was still lodged somewhere inside him. Another had grazed the top of his head, carving a bloody path across his scalp. The worst was the burst of rounds that peppered the left side of his ribcage. Sure, he'd been wearing a bulletproof vest, but the force of the impact had broken most of his ribs. Cruelest of all, he'd taken a round in his ass during his retreat. His right cheek felt like it had swollen to the size of a watermelon. His pants were soaked through with blood.

To add insult to all the injuries, Kimo had witnessed his boss, the supposedly fearless Seth Romero, retreated from the house on one of the gang's dirt bikes. The son of a bitch had abandoned them!

Kimo leaned over even more to spit out a mouthful of blood. The outlook was grim and getting more so by the minute. Yeah, there was a helicopter in front of the house, but even if he could make it there, he couldn't fly the damn thing. He lay down on the rough ground, feeling sorry for himself. He could hear footsteps approaching. Someone was crossing the lawn, heading straight for him. Maybe it was one of the feds following the trail of blood. Maybe it was the hot chick with the Uzi, coming to finish him off. It would be easy enough. Kimo was unarmed. He'd dropped his gun at some point during his retreat. He couldn't remember exactly when. Everything was a blur.

He closed his eyes and waited for whatever was coming. He heard the soft scrape of someone climbing over the stone retaining wall, then the soft thump of feet hitting the ground just beside him.

"Kimo!" The voice was hushed but the note of panic came through loud and clear. "No, you can't be dead. Kimo, please."

He opened his eyes and saw his sister crouched over him.

"Hey, sis," he groaned. "I'm not dead, but I'm...all fucked up..."

"You're going to be fine," Rosie insisted. "You're banged up, but you'll live."

Kimo forced a smile. Rosie had always been the strong one. "Yeah..."

"Listen, Harry is hiding somewhere in the house," she explained. "He knows how to fly the helicopter. If we can just get to the chopper, we can get out of here. Get you patched up and lay low until this fed investigation dies down. Then maybe we can head for the mainland. What do you think?"

"Sounds good," Kimo gasped. "But you better hurry. Don't think I can hold on much longer..."

Rowdy entered the house through a door on the north side. The plan was for Jade to go in through the south entrance and meet him in the middle. Whoever got to Edy first would get her the hell out of there. Any resistance they encountered along the way was to be met with deadly force. And that's why Rowdy went in with his four-barrel rocket launcher rather than the standard issue sidearm. If you were going to deal out kill shots, you'd better shoot with some degree of accuracy.

He made his way through the kitchen. From the looks of things, the rescue mission had interrupted breakfast. There were still cups of coffee on the counter, alongside plates of eggs, bacon, and toast. Rowdy figured that even lowlife criminals knew that breakfast was the most important meal of the day. He swiped a piece of bacon on his way past the counter and shoved it into his mouth. Even though it was cold, it was better than the oatmeal Donna had prepared that morning. The woman was a lot of things—a top-notch agent, a tough fighter, and a sexual dynamo—but no one would ever mistake her for a good cook. He thought about grabbing another piece but decided his appetite could take a back burner to the mission.

The bathroom next to the kitchen was empty. There was a discarded magazine lying on the floor next to the toilet, further evidence that their early morning raid had caught Romero's gang completely by surprise.

Rowdy turned away from the bathroom and went down a short hallway. The door at the end opened into a large, mostly empty room. The walls were adorned with taxidermy fish and framed photos of the Daioo family. Some of the photos were professional portraits, the kind of thing that close-knit families had taken on special occasions. Others were enlargements of snapshots from birthdays, picnics, or vacations. It was tragic to consider that a number of the people in those photos had likely come to a violent end at the hands of Seth Romero and/or his hired thugs. But that tragedy didn't concern Rowdy at the moment. What did concern him was that Edy St. James was standing in the middle of the room. Her arms were bound and held aloft by ropes that were anchored to the ceiling. She looked like a football referee signaling a touchdown. Her feet were also bound, held together at the ankles by the same rough rope. A piece of silver duct tape covered her mouth.

"Don't worry, Edy. I'm going to get you out of this," Rowdy assured her.

She jerked her head to the side, her eyes wide. Rowdy got the message loud and clear: they weren't alone. The door behind her creaked open, and one of Romero's gunmen stepped into the room with his pistol drawn and aimed right at Edy.

"Make one move and I'll kill her…"

Rowdy didn't hesitate. He didn't even bother to raise the rocket launcher to his shoulder. He squeezed the trigger, firing off a hipshot. In the fraction of a second between the trigger pull and the rocket's emergence from the barrel, the gunman's eyes grew wide. He didn't have time to speak, but he didn't need to. The expression on his face spoke volumes.

The impact of the rocket drove the man through the wall, smashing through the kitchen and exiting the roof. The detonation that followed was forceful enough to make the house's foundation tremble. Rowdy couldn't see the end result, but he knew the only way anyone would ever identify that poor son of a bitch was through dental records, and even that might be a stretch.

"Nice shooting, Tex," Jade said, stepping into the room.

"What can I say, it was a lucky shot." Rowdy pointed at Edy. "She's all yours, big guy."

Rosie hauled Harry through the back door. He stood on the patio, glancing around nervously. He wiped his hands on his denim shorts and licked his lips. This was bullshit. He'd been perfectly safe hiding in his bedroom closet when Rosie came charging in like a coked-up rhino and started barking orders at him. It didn't make sense. The gunshots coming from the front yard had slowed down. There were some sounds of fighting coming from the boss' karate room, but as far as Harry was concerned, that was none of his business. All they had to do was wait until the feds found their friend, then all this would be over. They just had to sit tight and wait. Then they could get the hell out of there and never look back. Hell, even the boss had taken off. No reason to hang around when even that psycho knew better than to fight it out with these feds. But just try telling Rosie that.

"Okay, where is he?" he asked nervously. "You said Kimo was out here, so where is he?"

"He's behind the wall." Rosie gestured toward the retaining wall that ringed the backyard. "Now get moving."

"You know I can't land that helicopter, right? I'm not even sure I can remember how to take off," Harry said, hating the whiny note that had crept into his voice. But Rosie had that effect on him. She was one scary broad. That routine with the nunchaku was pretty hot, he guessed, but it was also terrifying.

"We'll cross that bridge when we come to it." She grabbed his elbow and tugged him along. "You move like you got lead in your ass."

When they climbed over the wall and found Kimo lying in a bloody heap, Harry was sure the dude was dead. There was so much blood that it had turned the ground to sticky mud. Harry wrinkled his nose as his shoes squelched in it.

"I think he's..." Harry didn't want to finish that sentence, not with Rosie standing right there beside him.

"He's not," Rosie snapped. "He's not dead."

She knelt by her brother and coaxed him back to consciousness. He murmured groggily as she pulled his arm around her shoulders and slowly levered him upright.

"Okay," Harry said, "but how do you plan on getting to that chopper with those feds hanging around in the front yard? Not like they're just going to let us get away without a fight."

Rosie paused to consider. "Yeah, I guess you're right. We need some sort of diversion..."

They didn't have to wait long for a solution to present itself. They words had barely left Rosie's mouth when the front of the house exploded. The fireball that leapt into the air was like a sign from God.

"Come on!" Rosie shouted. "Let's go!"

Rowdy paused on his way out of the room to slap Jade a high-five.

"I'm going to make sure Donna and Taryn are okay," Rowdy said. "It sounds like the shooting has stopped, so maybe this operation is over and done with."

Jade nodded. "All over but the crying now."

Edy moaned behind her duct tape gag. Clearly, she was upset about something. Jade

sauntered across the room and stood in front of her, giving her a slow head-to-toe appraisal.

"You know, Edy, I think I dig this kinky stuff. Bondage is pretty hot," he said.

Edy rolled her eyes. She grunted insistently, gesturing with her hands as much as the ropes around her wrist would permit.

"Oh, baby," Jade said, smiling. "I hear you loud and clear. Just give me a minute to fetch the whips, chains, and midgets, then we'll get started. This is so exciting. I never thought it would happen to me."

Edy's brow furrowed.

"Okay, okay…" Jade dug his knife out of his pocket and got to work cutting the ropes binding her wrists. "Almost free, baby. Just give me a second…"

By the time he'd finished sawing through the ropes that bound her ankles, Edy had torn the duct tape off her mouth. That was a good thing too, because Jade figured he deserved a reward for all his heroism. Thankfully, Edy agreed. She grabbed him, twisting her fingers through his hair as she pulled him in for a kiss.

Rowdy didn't have a chance to collect any such reward from Donna. No sooner had he stepped out into the front yard than a firefight erupted. A trio of figures came around the corner of the house's west side, firing wildly as they beat a hasty retreat towards Romero's helicopter. Rowdy recognized them at once. Rosie and Kimo, aka The Terrible Twins, were two of Romero's most trusted hitters. Harry Kapua was small time muscle, a petty criminal who'd graduated from burglary and car theft to intimidation and murder under Seth Romero's tutelage. The agency had files on all of them.

Rosie was practically dragging her brother along. By the looks of things, Kimo had taken a few bullets during the morning's excitement. His skin—the few patches that weren't covered in blood—looked pale and ashen. His eyes were so heavy lidded that he appeared asleep. Harry Kapua appeared to be unharmed, but he also looked like he'd rather be anywhere else. His eyes were big and pleading, even as he swept the barrel of his Mac-10 back and forth, spraying bullets.

Rowdy dashed across the open space and took shelter behind the Jeep, where Donna and Taryn were crouched, waiting for their opportunity to return fire.

"Fancy meeting you here," he said, winking at Donna. "I mean, a nice girl like you in a place like this…"

"Not really the time, Rowdy." Donna popped up long enough to fire a crossbow bolt at the three figures. When she dropped back down, Taryn took a turn with her Uzi.

Since Rowdy heard no screams or explosions, he began to

suspect the ladies weren't finding their targets. This suspicion was confirmed by the sound of the helicopter's engine coming to life. The wind stirred by the rotors was growing stronger by the second, whipping up grains of sand that stung Rowdy's face.

"Give me that thing!" Donna shouted over the noise, pointing at Rowdy's rocket launcher. She ditched the crossbow, dropping it to the ground.

His clever remark about getting turned on by an assertive woman was lost in the steady *whup-whup-whup* of the whirling rotor blades. It was a shame, because Rowdy hated to waste such wit, but he passed the weapon to her with a smile. After all, there was more than a kernel of truth to the joke. It *did* get him hot when Donna got that serious look and started barking orders.

She shouldered the rocket launcher and stood up, shouting for the trio of scumbags to turn off the engine and exit the helicopter with their hands raised. Her order was answered with a staccato burst of gunfire. Rowdy peeked over the Jeep's hood and watched the helicopter begin a herky-jerky ascent.

"Who the hell is flying that thing, Ray Charles?" he wondered aloud, once again saddened that his one-liner was swallowed by the noise.

Donna shouted some more, but Rowdy knew it was pointless. He couldn't make out a single word she was saying, so there was a less than zero chance anyone inside that chopper could. Finally, Donna must have come to the same conclusion. Left with no choice, she pulled the trigger. A split second later, the helicopter exploded in a fireball so big Rowdy thought it might be visible from the mainland.

Taryn sprang to her feet, her mouth and eyes wide open in an expression of sheer wonderment.

"Holy shit!" she exclaimed. "That was just like that scene in *Live and Let Die*! Man, that was gnarly!"

Donna passed the rocket launcher back to Rowdy and shook her head. "Yeah, but that's just a movie. This is real life."

Taryn shrugged. "Yeah, I guess."

Donna slapped Rowdy on the shoulder then put her hands on her hips. "Are you going to back me up on this, numb nuts? Tell her this shit isn't the same as a movie."

Rowdy shrugged. "Hey, all I know is I love it when you talk dirty."

Donna glared at him for a moment, then the tension broke as they dissolved into laughter. Jade and Edy emerged from the house and picked their way through the wreckage. Hand-in-hand, they made their way over to the bullet hole-riddled Jeep.

"Looks like the gang's all here," Jade said. He looked over the front yard, surveying the smoking wreckage of the helicopter. "Now, that's some serious damage."

Donna grabbed Edy and pulled her into a hug. "Edy, I'm so sorry. Are you okay?"

"Oh, sure. No problem. I'm fine, thanks to you guys." Edy said, extracting herself from the embrace and pressing against Jade. She ran her hand over his chest and gazed into his eyes. "Especially you, you big sexy beast."

Taryn made a gagging sound. "I think I'm going to puke if I have to listen to this mush."

Despite the threat of imminent vomit, Jade and Edy shared a prolonged and very passionate kiss. Taryn made a big show of averting her eyes.

What the hell, Rowdy thought, *they've more than earned it.*

Donna cleared her throat. "I guess we're going to have to call this in to HQ. The bitching about paperwork is going to be long and loud, I'm sure. I can't wait to explain to the deputy director why there are bits of helicopter scattered all over this half of Molokai."

"This is nothing," Rowdy said. "You should have seen the aftermath of that operation in Baja two years ago."

"I'm glad you think this is entertaining," she replied. "What do you think, beers at my place? Maybe that phone call can wait until morning."

"Good idea," Jade said. "That'll give us time to get our stories straight."

Donna nodded, she stooped to pick up the crossbow. "I'm taking the ultralight, so I'll see you slowpokes when you get there."

"Just when I think you can't get any sexier, you grab a crossbow and start talking about beers." Rowdy sighed. "Agent Hamilton, you have stolen my heart."

Donna rolled her eyes. "You never stop, do you?"

Rowdy just smiled.

Chapter Twelve

The Jeep had been totaled by gunfire, so they hotwired one of Romero's vans. It was a real piece of shit, crammed full of an odd assortment of items: power tools, paint cans, suitcases full with clothes, a milk crate full of old records, boxes of moldy back issues of *Playboy* magazine, and a brand new Kawasaki dirt bike. They emptied out most of it, stacking the boxes and cases on the wreckage-strewn lawn, but Rowdy insisted on taking the dirt bike with them back to Donna's place. A nice bike like that, it would be a shame for it to be swept up in the agency's asset forfeiture program, where some bean counter would give it an appraisal before the suit and tie brigade stashed it in some warehouse.

It took Jade less than a minute's work with a screwdriver to break into the steering column and get the van started.

In the passenger seat, Edy applauded. "Wow, you made that look easy."

"Oh, it's nothing," Jade replied. "Just one of the many tricks I picked up during my childhood on the mean streets of Los Angeles. The gangs forced me to do terrible things. Stealing cars was the least of it."

"Oh, baby," Edy said, touching his arm. "I had no idea. You poor thing."

Rowdy laughed so hard he snorted. "He grew up in Palm Springs. The closest thing to gangs in his childhood were his three big sisters and the nuns at Catholic school."

Jade shrugged. "Details, my friend. Mere details. But hey, Edy, you wouldn't believe what happened back there. Rowdy fired six shots at one guy and missed every single time."

The van's engine backfired as soon as he put it in gear. The entire vehicle shuddered so violently that Rowdy thought whiplash might be a real possibility. By the time they made it to Donna's place, they might all be ready for neck braces.

"Hey, man," Rowdy said, slapping the back of Jade's seat. "I knew you'd cover me, amigo."

As soon as Jade wheeled the van off the Daioo property and onto the old two lane highway, Taryn began to chatter. Rowdy recognized her breathless yakking for what it was: the aftermath of combat adrenaline. It was something you saw all the time in rookie agents. Once the shooting was done, they rode high on the thrill until the reality of the situation set in. Then they either became giddy and talkative or got the shakes and puked up their guts. Since they were in an enclosed space, Rowdy offered up a silent prayer of thanks to whatever patron saint looked out for hotshot federal agents.

"That wannabe female bartender practically ran into my arms before I shot him," she gushed. "And man, did you see how Donna blew that helicopter to pieces? Before that, she shot, like, four dudes with a crossbow. A fucking crossbow! Can you believe it? She's so cool. I guess you guys did some damage too, huh? There was, like, an army of bad guys and we still managed to get the drop on them."

"Well, not to brag, but I did get to show off my martial arts expertise on Romero's hired ninja," Jade said. "Like I said, I don't want to sound like I'm bragging, but it was an impressive display."

"Hey, wait a second," Edy interrupted. "But did anyone happen to see that bastard Seth Romero today?"

Everyone went quiet for a moment. The van rumbled and shuddered its way over the potholed asphalt.

Edy finally broke the silence. "He was in that room with me when the shooting started. Then, all the sudden, he slapped that tape on my mouth and just took off. That was the last time I saw him."

Suddenly, Rowdy had a bad feeling in the pit of his stomach. Romero knew where Donna lived. Hell, the last time he'd paid her a visit, she'd shot him in the face. If he'd made the connection between her and the investigation into his criminal enterprise, there was only one place he could be headed. That bad feeling swelled. It was like he'd swallowed a frozen bowling ball. Romero was a purebred psycho, and they'd backed him into a corner. There was no telling what kind of evil shit he was capable of.

They were still miles from Donna's house. Taking into account the road conditions and the sorry state of the van, it was probably at least another fifteen minutes before they arrived. If only there was some way to get there faster, some way that didn't require a road…

"Hey, Jade," he said, slapping the back of the driver's seat. "Pull this hunk of junk over for a second."

Jade glanced back over his shoulder. "Why, you need to take a leak or something?"

"No, but I think it's time to take this dirt bike for a test drive."

The snake slithered through the darkness. Despite having a belly full of tourist meat, sleep had proved elusive. Normally, after a meal of that size, it would be overcome with a sluggish lethargy and slip into a deep sleep. But this time, the meal had seemingly endowed it with jittery, adrenalized energy. It slithered about the crawlspace in search of something new to explore. Panicked rodents and insects scattered at its approach, but the snake ignored them, driven on by an urge more primitive even than simple hunger.

It made a three complete circuits of the crawlspace before something caught its interest: the open end of a pipe. The narrow circle of darkness was enticing. The smells emanating from the opening were enticing and exotic. Forked tongue flicking, the snake poked its head inside. It found a moist warmth that was inviting. Although the space was narrow, the snake was steadily persistent and managed to work its way inside.

Its brain was too primitive for claustrophobia. It didn't panic in the space so narrow that the sides of the pipe pressed against its ribs. The snake simply flexed the muscles along the length of its body and inched forward, gradually nearing the light at the end of the tunnel.

Seth Romero ditched his dirt bike in the woods a half mile from Agent Donna Hamilton's house. He made the rest of the journey on foot, stealthily just in case the meddling federal agent had arrived before him.

Upon his arrival at the house, he discovered that he'd won the race. The ultralight aircraft was nowhere to be found, and there were no lights on in the house. He circled around to the back door. In his experience, it was always easier to break into a house through the back door. People put all their time and energy into fortifying the front of the house, but they rarely did much for the rear. That maxim held true, even for a federal agent as smart as this Donna Hamilton. The lock on the back door of her house gave up with a few pokes and prods from Seth's switchblade. He stepped into the quiet interior and surveyed his surroundings. He stalked from room to room, growing more impatient by the minute.

He wasn't angry, not anymore. He'd gone far beyond simple anger into unfamiliar emotional territory. The feeling that washed over him as he forced his way into the federal agent's house was something akin to calmness and clarity. For the first time in his life, he faced his circumstances with acceptance rather than angry defiance. His Molokai operation was in ashes, burned to the ground by a group of federal agents more driven and creative than any he'd before encountered. As soon as Mr. Chang received the news, he'd most likely dispatch someone to kill him. And this Hamilton broad, she was the driving force behind the whole thing. She was the engineer of his downfall. Seth couldn't help but admire her grit and determination. His admiration didn't change the fact that he would have to kill her. It was a moral imperative, if such a thing could exist in Seth's world of violence and crime.

It was easy enough to figure out which room was Donna's bedroom and which one belonged to the other broad. They were quite a pair, both of them with beautiful blonde hair and tits right out of a swimsuit calendar, and both of them as irritating and persistent as the foot fungus Seth had picked up from the shower at the local gym. But there were differences between the two women. The younger one—Seth didn't know her name—had living quarters better suited to a teenager than a federal agent. There were movie posters covering the walls. The vanity and the nightstand were heaped with tubes of lipstick, jars of face cream, and a thousand other makeup items Seth couldn't identify. A battery powered sexual device rested on the nightstand among all the cosmetics. Seth picked it up and gave it a sniff, then tossed it onto the bed and continued his tour of the house.

Donna's bedroom was neat and tidy. The walls were bare except for a framed photograph of a man with a distinguished profile and a meticulously trimmed mustache. Probably her father, Seth figured. Women like Donna Hamilton tended to idolize their fathers. Most likely, he'd been in law enforcement and she'd followed in his footsteps to win his approval. That sort of thing made Seth sick. He'd never had much use for family. After they'd immigrated to the United States from Cuba, his parents had become soft, law-abiding citizens. It was pathetic to witness.

Seth continued his inventory of the federal agent's room. He opened the drawers of her dresser one by one and pawed through the contents. He took his time with the undergarments, running his fingers over the panties and bras. It was mostly tasteful, no-nonsense stuff, but there were a few items that she most likely reserved for special occasions.

After he'd satisfied his curiosity, he sat on the edge of the bed and inhaled deeply, familiarizing himself with the scent of his prey. All that was left for him to do was wait.

Donna landed the ultralight in the front yard. The engine sputtered and coughed as she twisted the ignition. All things considered, the little aircraft had done just fine, but it was definitely due for a tune-up before the next flight. She made a mental note to have Glen Dickson's mechanics give it the full service as soon as possible.

She unbuckled the safety harness and climbed out of the pilot's seat. She stretched her stiff back muscles and took a deep breath. Now that the fighting was over, she felt as if a weight had been lifted from her shoulders. They'd managed to pull off Edy's rescue. In retrospect, it had been wild and reckless. During their debrief at the agency headquarters, they'd no doubt be treated to a reading of the riot act. Destruction of property wasn't viewed favorably, especially in a jurisdiction like Hawaii. Still, they'd struck a blow against the trafficking of dangerous narcotics through the islands, so there wouldn't be any real consequences. If anything, Taryn's participation in the rescue would work in her favor when it came to her training. Publicly, they'd be commended, of course. There would be plenty of photo-ops and glad-handing with every politician in the vicinity. Donna shuddered at the thought. She'd spent time around politicians before, and she'd hated every minute of it.

She went into the house through the front door and headed straight for the bathroom. At that moment, a hot shower sounded like a rare pleasure indeed. She twisted the knob and drew the shower curtain. While she waited for the water to heat up, she peeled off her clothes, stripping down to her panties.

"Not your best look, girlfriend," she said, examining her face in the mirror. Her hair was windblown and tangled, her face streaked with dirt. She gave her armpits a sniff and recoiled. "Twenty-four hour protection, my ass."

She turned back to check if the shower was ready, but froze as she heard the door creak behind her. There was no way Rowdy and the others had made it back already. The road from the Daioo estate to her house was a long, winding route, full of buckled asphalt and potholes. They couldn't have managed it that fast.

"I want my diamonds, bitch." The strangely accented voice coming from behind her dripped venom.

She turned and saw Seth Romero standing in the doorway. The bandage covering his wounded face was soaked through with blood. His eyes were those of a cornered animal. Bloodshot and open wide, the pupils shrunken to pinholes, they darted back and forth, like he was hoping to catch sight of the jewels somewhere in the bathroom.

He's completely insane, Donna thought.

Romero's lips pulled back from his teeth. He growled like a feral beast. His chest heaved as he panted.

Donna charged at him, putting her shoulder into his stomach and momentarily staggering him. She turned to run down the hallway, towards the front door, but he recovered too quickly for her to put any distance between them. He grabbed a handful of her hair and pulled her back. He pulled her into a backwards embrace, his arms wrapping around her ribcage just below her breasts. She stared at the switchblade in his clenched fist. The tip of the blade was mere inches from her chin.

"The diamonds," he growled, his breath hot and moist against the back of her neck.

"Fuck you!" She screamed, whipping her head backwards. She felt his nose crunch beneath the base of her skull.

His arms loosened enough for her to pull away, but he darted in front of her, putting himself between her and the front door. She feinted left, drawing him off balance just enough to give her the space to make a run for the closet. She wrenched open the door and threw herself inside, slamming the door behind her.

Romero howled with rage. His fists battered the door. Donna knew it was only a matter of moments before he broke through. She flipped the light switch and looked around desperately for something—anything—to use as a weapon. Her eyes fell on Taryn's spear gun. It was still loaded with barbed bolt. Donna prayed silently that the C02 canister sill had enough gas to fire it.

She grabbed the gun just as Romero's fist smashed through the insubstantial door. His arm snaked through the hole as he groped for the doorknob. He ripped open the door and stood there, chest heaving. Flecks of white foam flew from the corners of his mouth as he bellowed incoherently. Donna raised the spear gun to her shoulder and fired.

The bolt caught Romero in the chest, burying its barbed head deeply in the space just below his collarbone. He spun around, staggering into the living room like a drunk preparing to pass out. He fell to his knees, the switchblade falling from his hand as he grabbed the exposed portion of the bolt. He pulled at the blood-slicked metal shaft, but it refused to budge.

Donna dropped the gun and pounced on him, driving him

to the floor. He fell face-first, forcing the bolt even deeper into his chest as he thumped against the carpet. Donna scrabbled away from him, then planted her feet against his ribs and rolled him onto his back. He lay there motionless, his unblinking eyes staring up at the ceiling fan. Thick red blood oozed from the wound in his chest. Donna watched him for a moment, her body tensed. A minute crawled by before she felt safe enough to rise to her feet.

She shuffled into the kitchen and yanked open the freezer door. A sobering blast of cold air hit her square in the face. She grabbed the ice tray and broke a few cubes loose. Her hand trembled as she brought the ice cubes to her face and ran them over her overheated skin. Cold droplets rand down her cheeks and dripped onto the valley between her breasts. A sigh of relief died on her lips as she heard Romero gag and sputter as he rose from the floor. She turned just in time to see him lunge at her, switchblade clutched in his raised fist.

"I want my diamonds!" he shrieked, his voice ragged and raw. Blood and foamy saliva dripped from his open mouth. His features twisted into a hideous mask of bestial fury. He looked like something out of a horror movie, like some humanoid monster called into existence by black magic. Donna's worst nightmares couldn't have conjured a vision more terrifying.

She dropped the ice cubes and raised her arms to block his hand as he stabbed at her with the switchblade. She caught hold of his wrist and tried to force the blade away from her face. Her hand slipped, and the razor sharp blade slashed her palm as she struggled to maintain her grip. Blood ran down her arm and dripped onto the linoleum. Her muscles trembled with effort and he pushed her backwards until she was pressed against the refrigerator. All the while, the blade inched closer and closer.

Grunting with effort, she worked her left hand up to Romero's face. She tore away the bandage and dug her fingers into his wounded cheek. His eyes, already wide with animal rage, looked as if they might bulge right out of his skull. He howled as her fingers burrowed through his flesh until her nails scraped against his teeth. Still, he held onto the knife too tightly for Donna to wrest it away. Slowly, carefully, she let his hand get closer to her face. When his fist was within striking distance, she cocked her head to one side and bit down on his fingers.

No doubt her father would have called it a dirty move, but the bite did the trick. The knife slipped out of his hand. Donna made a blind grab for it, catching the knife as it fell. She held on as tightly as her bloody palm would allow. With one mighty heave, she forced him back just enough for her to bury the knife in his belly.

He staggered back a few steps, staring at the hilt of the knife. For a moment, Donna was sure that he was going to fall, but he managed to keep his balance. He seized the knife and tugged it free. Leering like a lunatic freshly escaped from the asylum, he came at her.

"Diamonds, bitch!" he wailed. "Diamonds...want..."

Donna sidestepped him and ducked into the bathroom. She instantly regretted the decision. There was nothing but a smashed door between her and Romero. And there was no escape route.

"Shit!" Donna screamed. All that tactical training and what did she do? Acted like a bimbo in a cheap horror movie. She giggled at the thought, because after all, it was a bit funny. She was practically naked, covered in blood, and doing her best to fight off a maniac with a knife. She looked exactly like a horror movie bimbo. Was this what they meant by life imitating art?

She fell backwards into the tub. Amazingly, the water spraying from the shower was still warm. Donna shook her head in disbelief. Of course it was still warm. The awful violence she'd just experienced had unfolded in a matter of minutes. Strange how it felt like hours.

Romero lurched into the bathroom. He stood beside the bathtub, gazing down at her and grinning like an idiot. Whether he was preparing himself to deliver one final line before stabbing her or was simply trying to catch his breath, Donna would never know. Before Romero could do anything other than raise his knife, the toilet exploded. Water sprayed upward like a geyser blowing its payload. Shards of porcelain flew like shrapnel through the air.

Donna turned her head to marvel at the cause of the explosion. Emerging through the opening in the floor where the toilet had sat only seconds ago was the biggest, ugliest snake Donna had ever seen. She recognized it instantly as the same snake that had been loaded onto her plane by mistake. The same snake that had escaped its crate in her garage. The same snake that had mutilated and partially devoured two young newlyweds from Indiana. That murderous mutant reptile was slithering its way out of the plumbing inch by terrible inch.

Romero's scream was so high-pitched and loud that Donna thought the mirror might shatter. It was the scream of someone witnessing his worst nightmare made flesh. He went on screaming until Donna was sure his vocal cords might snap, but he didn't move. Sheer terror had rooted him to the spot.

The snake responded with a sharp hiss, then launched itself at Romero. Its horribly distended jaws fastened onto his face, silencing his screams. It looked capable of swallowing his head in one gulp. With a swiftness that belied its massive girth, the snake wrapped itself around Romero's body. In a matter of seconds, he'd disappeared from sight, completely obscured by the coils of the monstrous reptile's body. Beneath its multicolored scales, the snake's muscles rippled as they contracted tighter and tighter. Donna heard a sound like twigs snapping and knew that the bones in Romero's body were being shattered one by one.

The snake wrenched its head to one side and turned its black-eyed, baleful gaze on Donna. In its jaws, it held Romero's severed head. Garlands of wet viscera dangled from the ragged stump of his neck.

Donna took a deep breath and did the only thing that seemed sensible in that moment. She screamed.

Rowdy dumped the dirt bike in the yard and sprinted toward the front door of Donna's house. The throaty rumbling of the bike's engine died away, replaced by the jagged notes of Donna's screams, which were climbing to operatic octaves. Hefting his four-barreled rocket launcher, Rowdy kicked the door open.

The scene inside that house was shocking, even for a man who'd seen many terrible things over the course of his career. There was blood everywhere. If it had been just that, Rowdy would have hardly taken notice. The true horror revealed itself to him as he made his way through the living room and into the hallway. There, in the doorway of the bathroom, was a snake so large and ugly that it defied reason. Rowdy's mind reeled, trying to make sense of what his eyes were seeing. The snake twisted its head around to stare back at him. A human head was held between its massive jaws. Rowdy recognized the head as having recently been attached to Seth Romero. Rowdy didn't know how to feel about that. On one hand, it was the most grotesque spectacle he'd ever beheld. On the other hand, it was almost comical in its absurdity. Either way, it was a fitting end for such a lowdown scumbag.

The snake's jaws clamped together, popping Romero's head like a grape. Brains dribbled from the snake's mouth as it swallowed. Rowdy's stomach lurched at the sight. The scene unfolding just a few feet away was enough nightmare fodder for a hundred sleepless nights. And just how the hell could he even begin to describe it in his report for the deputy director?

But just as quickly as his brain registered the shocking scene, Rowdy shoved his sense of revulsion aside. He could dwell on the gory details later. Right now, there was no time to waste. He shouldered his weapon, thanking God that he had one last rocket loaded. He took a deep breath and aimed carefully at the behemoth reptile.

"Gotcha," he whispered, squeezing the trigger.

The detonation was so forceful that Rowdy felt like he'd been punched in the chest. His heart fluttered. His ears rang. Bloody chunks of snake and human rained down around him, splattering every inch of the hallway.

Rowdy shrugged off his rocket launcher and charged through the carnage, his feet slipping and sliding through the coagulating puddles of gore. He entered the bathroom and found Donna waiting for him. A skimpy pair of bloodstained panties made up the entirety of her outfit. With a toss of her head, she cleared away the wet strands of hair that were plastered to her face.

"What took you so long?" she asked, smiling.

Rowdy stepped across the room and drew her into an embrace. Her body shook and trembled in his arms. He couldn't tell if she was laughing or crying or both. He held her until then tremors stopped, then gently pulled back.

"Where the hell did that snake come from?" he asked.

"Would you believe from the toilet?" Donna nodded to the empty space where the toilet had stood.

"Wow," Rowdy said, shaking his head. "Just when you thought it was safe to take a dump. Shame about the house. You're going to need some serious remodeling after this."

"Yeah, I guess so. But the shower still works." She hooked her thumbs into the waistband of her panties and tugged them down. "How about it, Mr. Action Hero?"

"Well, I'm covered in squishy bits of snake and drug dealing psychopath. I guess I could stand to take a shower."

Chapter Thirteen

"Okay, gang, what's on the agenda today?" Triple J asked, rubbing his hands together as he prepared to attack the plate of pancakes in front of him.

"I know you usually only cover sporting events," Taryn said, "but how'd you like to witness a real life arrest of the head of an international crime syndicate?"

Triple J paused with his fork halfway to his mouth. "Sounds like a whole lot of fun to me. Better than interviewing that Muffy Freemont again, anyway. You know what she told me? Her father had read that most accidents occurred within five miles of the home, so he moved the family to a new house exactly six miles away."

They were seated in the back corner booth at The Aloha Pancake Palace, getting an early dose of caffeine, sugar, and carbohydrates before the agents carried out a raid on the fourteenth floor of the Akuma building in downtown Honolulu. As far as raids went, it was going to be a low-key affair. Donna, Jade, and Rowdy would be the only federal agents present at the time of Mr. Chang's arrest. Taryn, Triple J, and Edy were along for the ride. The agents all agreed that their friends had earned the right to tag along. Well, maybe not Triple J, but Taryn had insisted that her boyfriend get a front row seat to the festivities. Edy had even sprung for a limo. She said they deserved to ride in style after all they'd been through.

"Tell you the truth," Rowdy said between bites of his western omelet, "I'm a little nervous to see this Mr. Chang in person. It feels a bit like going to shake hands with the devil."

Donna gave him a look. "Okay, you're going to have to explain. What's the big deal with this guy? And from the photo you showed me, it looks like he's a white guy. Why's he named Chang anyway?"

"Damien Chang was born in Hong Kong," Rowdy explained. "His mother was British and his father was Chinese. Oxford educated. He's suave and cultured, but he's also merciless and sadistic. Try this one on for size: his personal bodyguard is a guy named Anatoly Rassimov. He's better known as Destroyer."

"Hey, wait…" Triple J paused his destruction of his full stack with extra bacon on the side to think. "That name, Anatoly Rassimov sounds familiar."

"He used to be a professional wrestler," Jade said. "Killed two men in the ring. First one was ruled an accident, but the second one got the authorities looking into him. He split town before they could make an arrest. After retiring from the ring, did some work for the New York mob, mostly breaking legs for loan sharks. Then he graduated up to wetwork, whacking anyone who threatened to turn state's witness. Eventually, he got tired of the Big Apple and headed overseas to work for Chang."

"Basically, what Rowdy is saying, is that this Chang dude isn't a very nice guy," Jade said. "I also hear his table manners are terrible. Elbows on the table and everything."

Taryn looked across the table at Donna. "You guys got a plan for dealing with that sort of monster?"

"You know what they say," Donna replied, "the bigger they are, the harder they fall."

She held up her right hand, still bandaged from its encounter with Seth Romero's switchblade. She partially unwound the bandage to reveal a pair of brass knuckles.

"That's my girl," Rowdy laughed. "Now eat up so we can get this show on the road."

It took Triple J exactly two minutes to polish off his breakfast and devour what was left of everyone else's. The meal was on the house, courtesy of Edy's connection to the owner of the restaurant, but everyone laid out cash to tip the waitress. Then they headed out to the parking lot, where the limo driver was waiting on them.

There was a guard stationed at the front door of the Akuma building. When he asked for ID, Rowdy and Donna flashed their badges.

"Holy shit," the guard said, his eyes wide. "You guys about to bust someone?"

"What do you think?" Rowdy asked.

He and Donna headed for the elevators before the guard could answer. The stepped into the first available car headed up.

"I asked a guy from one of our surveillance teams to do a little recon for me," Rowdy explained to Donna as he stabbed the button for the fourteenth floor. "I had him keep an eye on the building once I figured out it was where Chang was laying his head. According to my guy, it's just Chang and his pal Destroyer up there. We get lucky, maybe we catch them still eating breakfast and they go quietly."

Donna raised her eyebrows. "And if they kick up a fuss?"

Rowdy laughed. "I think you know the answer to that."

The elevator reached its destination and the doors whooshed open. Rowdy led the way to the corner penthouse. The door didn't look like much. In a building like this, rich people didn't need much front door security. That was part of the allure. Up here, they were insulated from the rabble. Nobody who was allowed up here would ever dream of stealing from one of the residents.

Rowdy paused in front of the door. He looked at Donna and raised his hand with his fingers splayed. He mouthed a silent countdown from five to one, then raised his foot and applied it to the door with as much strength as he could muster. The door rewarded his effort by swinging open without complaint. Rowdy stepped into the apartment with Donna following close behind.

"Man, would you take a look at this place." Rowdy shook his head.

"I guess crime *does* pay in the short term," Donna said. "But in the long term, it ends up costing much more."

"You should put that on a bumper sticker," Rowdy suggested.

There was a closed door just ahead and to their right. They opened it and stepped into the room without bothering to knock first. Rowdy figured that serving an arrest warrant wasn't exactly an occasion that called for social graces. The room was some sort of office. A desk made of darkly stained hardwood was the centerpiece. It sat atop an intricately-patterned Oriental rug. Two wingback leather chairs in front of the desk accounted for the rest of the furniture. The walls were decorated with the same Asian motifs as the rest of the apartment. A rack of katana sword hung on one wall, and a suit of samurai armor stood in the corner. The room was equal parts stuffy British refinement and Far East mysticism.

Mr. Chang sat behind the desk. Behind him was a floor to ceiling window offering a panoramic city view. Beside him was an oversized human that Rowdy assumed was Destroyer.

"Please, won't you have a seat?" Mr. Chang gestured to the chairs.

"I think we'll stand if it's all the same to you," Rowdy replied.

"As you wish."

Rowdy reached into his back pocket and pulled out a folded square of paper. He tossed it on the desk. "Here's a little treat for you. It's a federal arrest warrant. And just so we're clear about what's going on here, I'm going to give you the formal version. Damien Chang, you are under arrest for trafficking narcotics, facilitating the murder of law enforcement officers, and criminal acts too numerous to recite. All the details are in the paperwork. I'm sure your lawyer will put them in terms even a scumbag like you can understand. The short version is that you've been a very bad boy. INTERPOL is all hot and bothered to extradite you to the old country, but since you're here, Uncle Sam gets first crack at you. Now, stand up and place your hands on top of your head."

Mr. Chang cut his eyes sideways and snapped his fingers. "Destroyer, tear them in half."

Destroyer smiled. He rolled his head around on his massive shoulders and cracked his knuckles. He stepped around the desk and gave Rowdy a shove.

"Come on, pig," the bodyguard sneered. "You going to pull out your gun and shoot me or you going to fight like a man?"

Rowdy took a step back. "Oh, I think maybe I'd rather fight like a girl this time."

The answer seemed to confuse Destroyer. Apparently, there weren't a lot of brains in that thick skull. "What's that supposed to mean?"

Rowdy smiled. He raised his hands in a classic boxer's pose.

"Oh, really?" Destroyer laughed.

Rowdy drew back his fist like he was preparing to swing a haymaker right at the bodyguard's iron jaw. Then he abruptly shifted his weight, drew back his foot, and kicked Destroyer square in the balls. The giant's eyes grew so wide Rowdy thought they might pop out of his head. Destroyer doubled over, hands pressed to his crotch. Rowdy kneed him in the face, breaking his nose and loosening a few teeth. Donna stepped in and punched Destroyer in the back of the head. The brass knuckles made contact with the base of his skull, and just like that, the dreaded Destroyer's lights went out. He collapsed, to the floor face-first, cracking his forehead on the edge of the desk as he went. Blood soaked the expensive carpet.

Rowdy had seen enough fights to know when a guy was down for the count. Destroyer wouldn't be engaging in any acts of violence anytime soon.

"As I was saying…" Rowdy whipped out a pair of hand-cuffs. "Damien Chang, you are under arrest. Come on, don't give me that look. This is over and you know it."

"In a pig's ass!" Mr. Chang sprang up from his desk. He looked like an angry toddler, his face bright red and his lower lip trembling.

Rowdy gave Donna a look. "Did he just say 'in a pig's ass'?"

Donna shrugged. "Maybe it's a British thing?"

Mr. Chang rushed to the wall and grabbed one of the katana swords from the rack. He unsheathed the blade and raised it.

"Okay, Mr. Chang, that's just stupid," Rowdy said, drawing his pistol from the holster on his belt. "Don't you know better than to bring a knife to a gun fight?"

Donna reached into her jacket and drew her own weapon. The gun was a nickel-plated Desert Eagle, so comically over-sized in her hand that Rowdy had to stifle a laugh. Leave it to Donna to go overboard, bringing a .50 caliber hand canon to the arrest of a 60-year old man who couldn't have gone more than a buck-fifty soaking wet.

"Go ahead," Donna said. "Make my day, you cop-killing piece of shit."

Mr. Chang charged, bellowing a war cry. Donna and Rowdy fired their weapons simultaneously. Rowdy's shot went wide of the mark, blowing a hole through the window behind Mr. Chang. Donna's shot, however, was a bullseye. The .50 caliber bullet punched right through Mr. Chang's chest. And since an undersized drug kingpin offers little in the way of resistance, the bullet kept on going, putting another hole in the window. The force of the impact lifted Mr. Chang off his feet, throwing him against the window. Weakened by the two bullet holes, the glass cracked in a spider web pattern. For a single sickening second, it looked like the safety glass might hold, but then, with a sound like crumpling plastic, it gave way. Mr. Chang's body toppled backwards and plummeted to the ground.

Rowdy and Donna holstered their guns, then stepped over Destroyer's unconscious bulk and peered over the edge of the window frame. Mr. Chang's body was a bloody mess on the sidewalk. Taryn, Triple J, Edy, and Jade stood around it in a semicircle, shaking their heads in dismay.

Rowdy pulled Donna away from the window and guided her back into the hallway.

"Thanks for being so quick on the draw, kiddo," he said as they waited for the elevator to arrive. "I could have taken ten shots and still missed the son of a bitch."

She slipped an arm around his waist. "So what if you can't aim? You have other redeeming qualities."

Chapter Fourteen

The week after Damien Chang's death went by in a blur of interviews, depositions, and debriefing sessions. Once the deputy director had finally closed the book on the operation, calling it "flawed from a procedural standpoint, but otherwise a success," the principal actors—Rowdy, Jade, Donna, Taryn, Edy, and, along for the ride once again, Triple J—caught a flight out of Honolulu. At Rowdy's invitation, they were all going for a cruise on the *Malibu Express* to decompress. Nothing but pleasant days at sea with plenty of champagne, from Malibu all the way to Cabo San Lucas.

Their first evening aboard, the entire gang gathered on the aft deck to sip cocktails and watch the sunset.

Rowdy raised his glass and offered a short toast. "Here's to good friends and the downfall of an international criminal enterprise. Let's drink up and have fun. I'd say we've more than earned it."

"I agree," Taryn said before tossing back her drink on one gulp.

After taking a modest sip of her drink, Donna spoke up. "I hate to be the wet blanket here, but shouldn't we go back to Molokai and start searching for the other box of diamonds? I

173

mean, officially it's presumed lost, but we have to turn it over to the agency sooner or later."

There were reluctant murmurs of agreement all around, except from Taryn who shook her head and raised a hand for silence.

"Just hold your horses, everyone," she said. "But *we* don't know where the diamonds are."

Edy shook her head. "I don't get it."

Taryn laid a hand on her chest. "Only *moi* knows where the diamonds are. Before we packed up to make the trip here, I went out to that field by the Daioo estate and spent a couple hours crawling around in the grass. You wouldn't believe the sort of things you can find if you look hard enough."

"Is she saying what I think she's saying?" Jade asked.

"Let me spell it out for you," Taryn continued. "As federal agents, you're required by law to turn in any confiscated goods, right?"

Rowdy nodded. "That's correct."

"Well, as you know," Taryn said, "I'm still just a mere civilian as far as the agency is concerned. And since anyone who could positively identify the diamonds is dead, the diamonds belong to me."

"Now, hold on a minute," Triple J said. "I'm just a dumb jock, but can she really do that?"

"She sure can," Rowdy answered, a sly smile spreading over his face.

"And," Donna added, "she's perfectly entitled to share that newfound wealth with her friends."

Taryn nodded. "A job worth doing is a job worth doing at the right price."

Rowdy raised his glass again. "I'll drink to that."

The following pages feature images from the film *Hard Ticket to Hawaii*. Used by permission.

HARD TICKET TO HAWAII
TELE 5 PRÄSENTIERT SCHLEFAZ - DIE SCHLECHTESTEN FILME ALLER ZEITEN OLIVER KALKOFE & PETER RÜTTEN
ERNST KRAMER SVEN KNOCH JANA KÖNIG OLIVER KALKOFE & JÖRG STROMBACH
EINE KALK TV PRODUKTION IN COPRODUKTION MIT fairworks IM AUFTRAG VON 5
THAT'S ALL FOLKS! BUT IT'S NOT THE END!

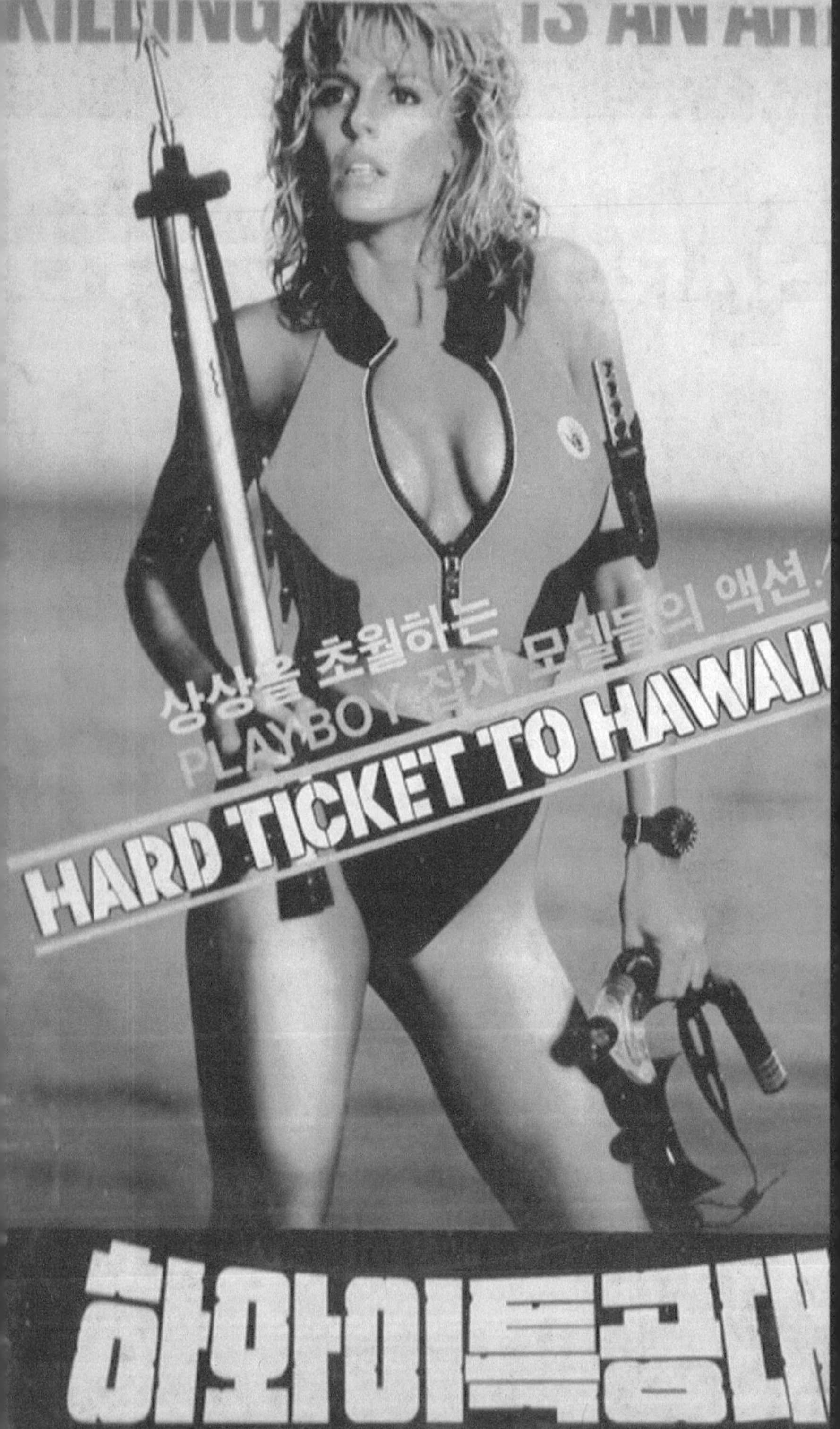

KILLING IS AN ART
상상을 초월하는
PLAYBOY 잡지 모델들의 액션
HARD TICKET TO HAWAII
하와이특공대

ALA MOANA
YACHT
CLUB
HONOLULU

MALIBU EXPRESS

MOLOKAI
COUNTY
MARSHAL

HARD TICKET TO HAWAII

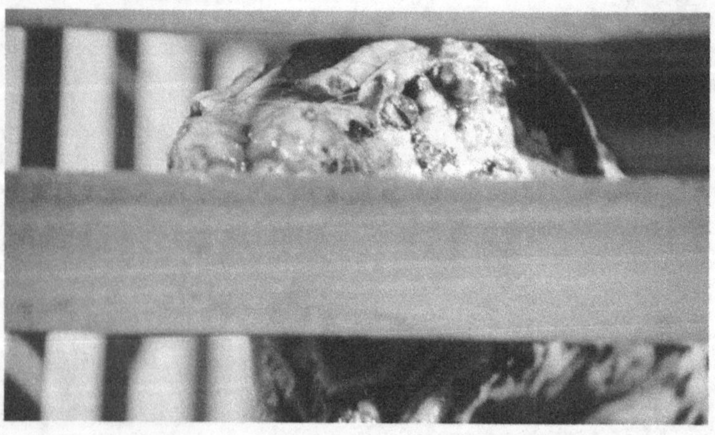

CAUTION!
LIVE SNAKE

BOAS
CAUTION!

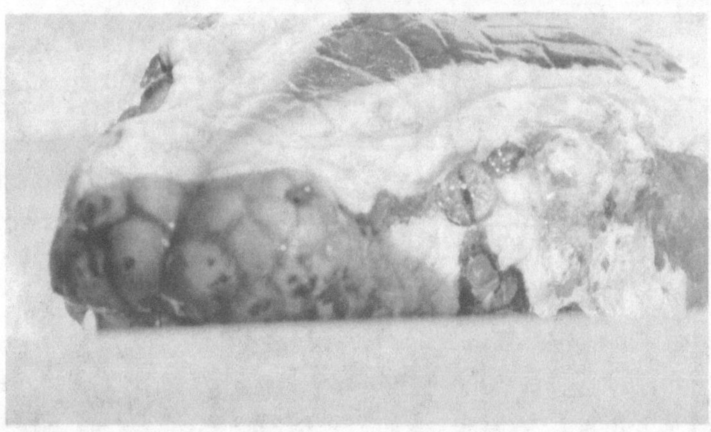

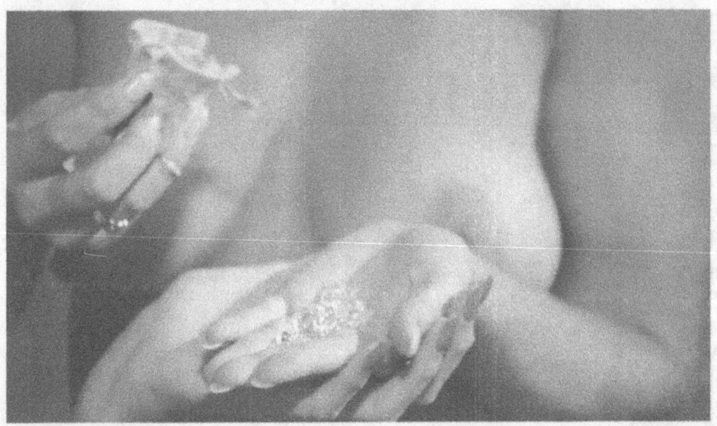

SEVEN
SUPER-PROFIS
WILLIAM SMITH IN
SEVEN die SUPER-PROFIS

SEVEN
die
SUPER-PROFIS

MALIBU
EXPRESS

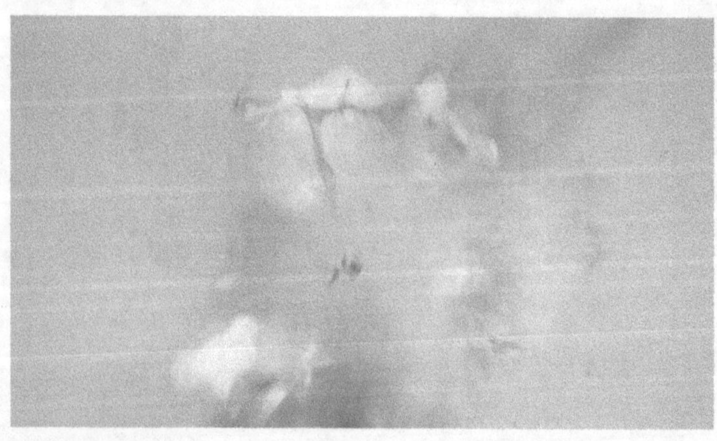

Molokai Cargo

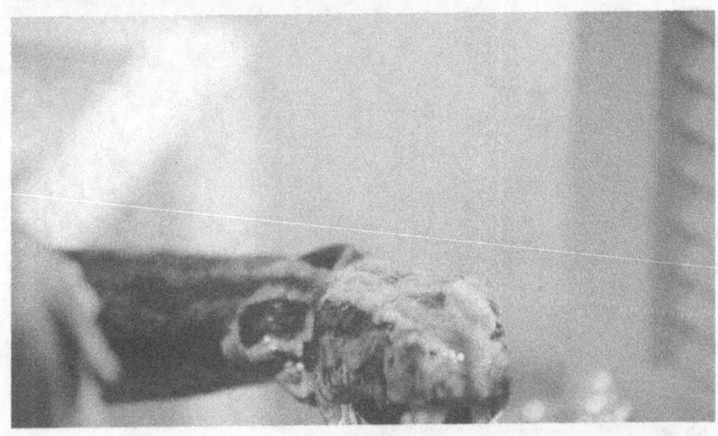

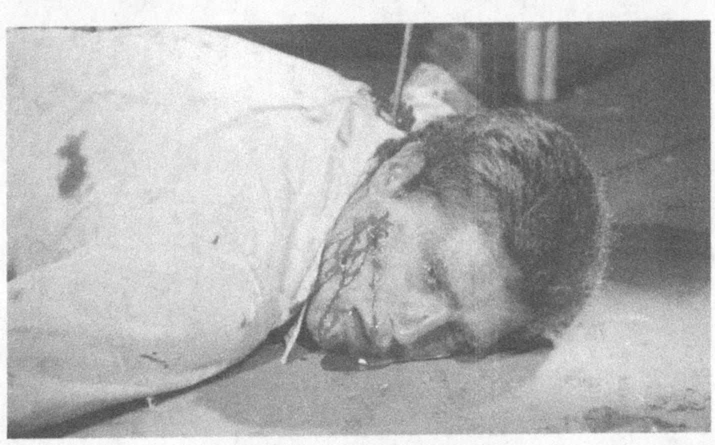

MALIBU EXPRESS

THE END

About the Author

Brad Carter lives in Arkansas with his wife and daughters. They encourage him to write, because it keeps him out of trouble.

Also from Brad Carter
(dis)Comfort Food
Saturday Night of the Living Dead
Only Things
Uncle Leroy's Coffin
Human Resources
Cruel Jaws
Rats: Night of Terror
Virus: Hell of the Living Dead
Malibu Express